No Time To Cry

Lurlene McDaniel

Cover design by Michael Petty

Published by Willowisp Press
801 94th Avenue North, St. Petersburg, Florida 33702

Printed in the United States of America

4 6 8 10 9 7 5

ISBN 0-87406-637-9

Dawn staggered to the bathroom, convinced that a warm shower would make her feel better. But when she shed her nightgown and looked into the mirror, her heart wedged in her throat. A fine red rash covered her arms and torso.

She started shaking so violently that she had to grab hold of the sink for support. She knew what the rash meant—she'd read too many medical booklets following her transplant. A rash was often the very first sign of bone marrow rejection.

One

"**H**EY Dawn . . . Dawn Rochelle! Wait up."

At the sound of her name being called in the jammed hallway, Dawn stopped suddenly and was almost mowed over by a group of kids hurrying to classes. She flattened herself against the bank of lockers and waited for her friend Rhonda to struggle through the crowd.

"Is this a mob scene or what?" Rhonda half-shouted above the noise.

"I never expected the first day of high school to be so crazy," Dawn admitted. "I think everybody's lost—even the seniors." Since she and Rhonda were only sophomores, they had expected to be hunting for every room on their assignment cards. But Hardy High was brand new and no one had attended classes there yet. Everyone seemed to be bewildered by the maze of halls and doors that looked all alike.

"According to the info packet, green room numbers mean science; red, math; brown, language; blue, the arts—"

"Enough already!" Dawn interrupted her friend. "Let's see if we have any classes together before the first bell rings."

They compared their schedules. Dawn was disappointed that the only class she and Rhonda shared was a final period Driver's Education class. They wouldn't even be in the lunch room at the same time. "I hate to admit it," Rhonda said, "but I miss our dinky old junior high school."

"Me too. At least we knew our way around."

"And we knew everybody and everybody knew us."

Dawn glanced around at the kids bustling through the hallway and realized that except for Rhonda, she didn't know a soul. In June, she'd been looking forward to attending a school where she could be anonymous, where most of the kids wouldn't know what the previous three years of her life had been like. She was tired of kids whispering behind her back and pointing to "that girl who has cancer."

Now, after the long summer she'd been through—her experience at cancer camp as a counselor, her months being a friend to Marlee, one of girls in her cabin, of visits to Marlee in the hospital and watching the young girl die—now she longed to put the past behind her and be a normal girl with a normal life. That is, if there were such a thing for a victim of leukemia.

"I'm glad we're taking Driver's Ed together," Rhonda said.

"I'm just glad your parents are letting you get your permit at all," Dawn answered. Rhonda could have gotten her permit last year when she was a freshman, but her parents made her wait until she brought her grades up.

The blast of an electronic bell warned that classes would soon begin. Dawn quickly glanced at her card. "I've got English upstairs. Do you suppose that's a brown room number?"

"Beats me. I'm trapped in biology. Definitely green."

Both girls laughed. "See you last period," Dawn called as Rhonda scampered off.

Dawn made her way to the stairwell. She clutched her new notebook to her chest and tried to stay out of everyone's way. A group of boys wearing letter jackets—football players, she guessed—sauntered past her. One of them gave her the once-over, and her cheeks flushed bright red. His interest made her feel good in one way, but in another way, she wondered what his reaction might be if he knew she'd had cancer.

She thought of her brother, Rob. He'd played football once, but a knee injury in his sophomore year had ended his career. Now he was at Michigan State finishing his senior year. He was graduating early, in December, and Dawn was sure he'd be coming home. After all, Katie was still here, and anyone could tell that Rob was head-over-heels in love with nurse Kate O'Ryan.

"Watch where you're going!"

The sharp words drew Dawn up short. "Sorry," she mumbled, steering clear of a girl who was busy arranging information on a bulletin board.

"Probably sophomore sludge," Dawn heard the girl mutter under her breath.

Dawn tossed her head of thick auburn hair, attempting to shake off the girl's hurtful words. *Well, I wanted to start fresh*, she told herself. *Guess I'll have to put up with an insult or two.*

By the time she hooked up with Rhonda in the Driver's Ed room that afternoon, Dawn was relieved to see a familiar face. So far that day, she'd gotten lost twice, and it was hard not to feel overwhelmed by all the new faces. Although she'd seen a couple of her former classmates, always at a distance, she realized that the juggling of the school district lines had truly put her and Rhonda in another world, but in a way she was relieved. Now she wouldn't have a bunch of people asking her about her health all of the time.

"I've got the cutest guy in my French class," Rhonda blurted the moment Dawn slid into the desk next to her. "How about you? Any hunks?"

"I didn't notice," Dawn confessed.

"You didn't *notice*? Why not? Isn't that what high school's all about?"

"Silly me. I thought it was to take classes, get good grades, and prepare for college."

Rhonda rolled her eyes in exasperation. "Maybe I'd feel that way too if I had a gorgeous guy like Brent Chandler waiting in the wings, but I don't."

"Don't start on that. I told you he and I were only friends." Brent had called her from West Virginia the week before to say that he was on his way to West Virginia Tech for freshman orientation. "You will write to me, won't you?" he'd asked.

"You bet," she had assured him. Brent was handsome and nice, and they'd had a wonderful time together at camp. But she wasn't kidding herself. She figured that a high school sophomore couldn't possibly hold much interest for him once he was settled on campus. Dawn knew that it was their shared memories of his sister Sandy that had brought them together in the first place. But, like Marlee, Sandy was dead. Sandy, her best friend ever. And Dawn was left to carry on with everyday life.

"Well, then if you and Brent are only friends, all the more reason to check out the guys here at Hardy," Rhonda insisted. "The first football game is Friday night, and there's a dance afterward in the gym. I think you and I should go."

"Are you asking me for a date?"

Rhonda gave Dawn a murderous look. "Very funny. I'm just saying it would be fun to go and hang around and check out the prospects. What do you say?"

"Can we talk about this later?"

A teacher entered the room and wrote

"Mr. De Marco" on the board. Then he explained, "We've got eight weeks of classroom work, then we'll put it into practice in the driving area next to the school track. Each of you will drive solo with me, and if you pass all parts of the class, you can take your driving test when your birthday comes up."

"Freedom," she heard Rhonda sigh.

Freedom. Dawn wondered what it was like. Ever since she was thirteen, her life had revolved around leukemia. Hospitals, chemo treatments, remission, check-ups, relapse, a bone marrow transplant, more check-ups. She felt as if she'd spent forever fighting the monster that had invaded her body two and a half years before. But the battle scars were mostly on the inside. Surely, nothing showed on the outside now that she was going on sixteen and in total remission.

Her gaze darted around the room. Could any of the kids sitting in the class really tell what she'd been through by simply looking at her? And how would they treat her if they knew? She felt as if she'd been forced to grow up far too fast. She'd hardly had a chance to be a kid. Dawn promised herself right then that all that was truly

11

behind her. She wanted her life back. And she didn't want to share it with anything having to do with cancer.

Two

"HOW was your first day?" Dawn's mother asked the moment she arrived home from school.

"It was fine, Mom." Dawn tossed her books on the kitchen counter and poked through the contents of the refrigerator.

"Don't spoil your supper."

"I won't." She took out an apple and bit into it, savoring the juicy sweetness. There had been times when she was so sick from chemo that she couldn't keep anything down, and other times, when she'd been taking cortisone drugs, that she couldn't get enough to eat.

"Tell me about it," her mom coached.

"I got lost a lot. Rhonda and I have Driver's Ed together. There's a football game Friday night."

"That's it, huh?"

13

Dawn wished her parents didn't expect her to spill her guts over every detail of her life. Didn't they realize that she liked her privacy? Instantly, she felt ashamed. She still had to take certain chemo medications and immune-suppressant drugs to keep her body from rejecting Rob's bone marrow. Her parents had stood by her through the worst of her ordeal. She knew she never would have made it without their support.

She smiled contritely. "Hardy's awfully big and I felt like a lost sheep most of the day. Except for Rhonda, I don't have any friends. The juniors and seniors all seem to have their own groups, and new kids aren't exactly invited in."

"I'm sure they'll warm up to you as time goes by. Are there any after-school activities that might appeal to you? Cheerleading?"

Dawn had been a cheerleader in seventh and eighth grade, but hadn't been able to keep up with the practices when she was in and out of the hospital. "Cheerleading's different in high school," she said. "You have to try out in the spring."

"Maybe next year," said her mother. "Anything else?"

Dawn toyed with the stem of her apple. "I'm not sure what I want to do."

"You're taking college prep courses. Maybe there's something fun for college-bound students."

"I have no idea what I want to study in college. My future's one big mystery."

"Something will come along that you'll like," her mother said cheerfully. She picked up a potato from beside the sink and started peeling it as she talked. "By the way, Katie called to remind you of your clinic appointment tomorrow at four."

Dawn felt the familiar twinge of apprehension. She'd been going for bloodwork regularly since her bone marrow transplant. And even though she had received a good report each time, she always felt a shiver of fear before every test. What if her white blood cell count was elevated? What if Rob's bone marrow stopped working and her leukemia returned? What if she had a severe episode of rejection?

"Did you hear me?" her mother asked.

"Of course I heard you." Dawn said peevishly.

"I'll pick you up from school at 3:30 and take you."

"I can grab a bus."

"Oh, honey, that's silly. I'll come and get you."

Stop treating me like a baby! Dawn had to bite her tongue to keep from saying it aloud.

"Katie wants to show you something," her mother said, smoothing over the awkward moment. "She says she'll bring you home."

"What's she want to show me?"

"She didn't say, but she was eager for you to see it. I invited her to stay for dinner tomorrow night." Dawn's mother sighed. "I know she misses Rob as much as he misses her. Maybe seeing us will help. I was a little worried that he might not want to finish up at Michigan State because it would mean they'd be apart for four months."

Dawn dropped her apple core into the trash. "Not too far apart," she said. "Rob told me he'd be home once a month no matter what."

"Love," her mother mused with a smile. "Isn't it wonderful? I can't believe that this is the same boy who washed his face because some girl kissed him at a birthday party. Of course, he was nine then."

Dawn suddenly remembered how badly Marlee had wanted to be kissed just once before she died. *"For real. Not like in my dream*," she'd told Dawn. It seemed like such a small wish. Now it would never come true.

She wondered how Marlee's grandmother was doing without her granddaughter around. Mrs. Hodges had raised Marlee and then lost her to cancer. Her own health was poor, and Marlee's hospitalization had been difficult on her.

Dawn told herself she should call the elderly woman and say hello. She'd looked so lost and alone after Marlee's funeral. But although Dawn went up to her room and even picked up the phone receiver, she didn't call. This was her first day of school and the start of a brand new year. All she wanted to do was leave the past behind and look to the future.

* * * * * *

The next morning, Rhonda called in a panic. "Can you believe it? I overslept. Anyway, you'll have to walk to the bus stop without me. Mom will run me to school."

"See you in Driver's Ed," Dawn replied, feeling slightly dismayed as she hung up the phone. She didn't have anybody to sit with on the bus and wasn't looking forward to boarding it alone. *Grow up!* she told herself. After all, she'd never been one to travel in groups. It was another habit she'd missed out on because she'd been busy having cancer instead of collecting groups of friends. Being sick meant spending a lot of time by yourself.

When she was thirteen and diagnosed with leukemia, she'd felt like a freak. She'd looked like a freak, too, after all her hair fell out and sores had broken out on her skin. She'd worn scarfs and wigs to hide her baldness. In school, there had been plenty of kids who treated her as if she were contagious and stayed far away from her, but she'd had some good, loyal friend through it all. Rhonda had been one. Rhonda wasn't a friend like Sandy, of course. Only someone who'd been through hospitalization and chemo could truly understand what life with cancer was like.

Sandy had been through it all, Dawn reflected. She'd been there when Dawn first found out about her own cancer—barely thirteen and suddenly thrust into a world of pain and fear and confusion. Sandy had only been in the hospital two weeks herself, but she was a pillar of strength and reassurance for Dawn. Always optimistic, always encouraging. They'd learned about leukemia together—about staying positive and battling the cancer cells through imaging. They'd been through chemo together; their hair had even fallen out at the same time!

Dawn sighed wistfully. She would always miss Sandy. It seemed so unfair that their time together had been so short.

Her thoughts were interrupted by the phone ringing again. She stared blankly at it for a moment before reaching over to answer it.

"Me again!" Rhonda's cheerful voice snapped her back to the present. "Forgot to ask you—did you ask if you could go to the game and the dance Friday night?"

"Yep. I can go."

"Good. We'll have to figure out what to wear to impress the guys."

"Don't you ever give up about boys?"

"No way. This is my year. I can feel it."

Dawn was still smiling to herself over Rhonda's optimism while she walked to the bus stop. Overhead, the trees were still green, but Dawn could already feel the autumn in the air. In another few weeks, the weather would turn nippy and the leaves would begin to change color.

She hadn't gone far down the block when she began to notice a car following her. *It's your imagination*, she told herself. But it soon became obvious that it wasn't. The car was some weird shade of bronze. It was old, and its muffler was loud. Her heart began to beat faster.

The car pulled alongside her, and for an instant she considered bolting and running. The driver, a teenage boy, leaned across the passenger seat and slightly out the window. "Dawn?" he asked. "Dawn Rochelle? Is that you?"

Dawn stopped cold in her tracks and peered at him suspiciously. He looked familiar, but she couldn't see his face very well. How did he know her name? Taking a step closer, she could see that he had black hair and deep brown eyes—the color of rich chocolate. Suddenly she realized why he looked familiar.

"*Jake?*" she whispered.

His face broke out into a dazzling smile. "Yup, it's me—Jake Macka. Don't you recognize me?"

Three

Jake Macka! Memories of the past tumbled through her mind like scenes from an old movie. "Is it really you?" *Dumb question!* she told herself. Her heart thudded and her knees felt weak. "But you moved away almost two years ago." She instantly recalled how disappointed she'd felt when his family had left Columbus. It was just before her relapse.

"Well, a year and a half ago, actually. But my dad's company moved him back last month. We've got a house over on Claremont Avenue. I'm going to Hardy High. You too?"

"Yes."

"Hop in. I'll drive you." He reached over and opened the passenger side door.

Dawn thought for just a second about what her parents would say. But they knew

Jake and his family, so she figured it was okay to accept his offer of a ride. She climbed into the car, still numb with the shock of seeing him. She'd had a crush on Jake in the fifth grade that had lasted until he moved. Now, seeing him again, after more than a year, she could hardly think straight. He was taller, more muscular, and his shoulders were broader, but he had the same heart-melting smile and warm brown eyes that had always sent chills through her.

"When I saw you walking along the sidewalk, I couldn't believe it was you," Jake said. "I told myself, 'It's just someone who looks like Dawn.' But the longer I looked, the more I was sure it was you. It's the hair. I always thought you had the prettiest color hair." She touched her shoulder-length hair self-consciously. "You look great," Jake said, easing the car into traffic. "How are you?"

"I'm fine."

He pulled up at a stoplight and studied her carefully.

"No, I mean how are you, *really?*"

Of course, Jake would remember her first hospitalization and diagnosis. Her entire class had sent her get-well cards, including an unsigned one with an adorable teddy bear on the front, which she'd always suspected was from him.

"I heard you had a bone marrow transplant."

"You did?"

"One of your friends called and left a message about it. I called you, but I guess someone forgot to tell you."

Dawn vaguely recalled an entry Rob had made in her diary, when she was too sick to write in it herself, about calls from lots of friends. Jake had been one of them.

She felt a warm tingling sensation all the way down to her toes. Still, the last thing she wanted to discuss with him now was her health.

"The doctors think I'm cured," she said breezily, hoping to end the discussion.

His face broke into a smile. "That's terrific! I'd never known anyone with cancer and I thought you were brave—a real hero."

"Not me," she said with a self-conscious laugh. "You were the hero."

"When?"

"When you ran for the touchdown and Adams beat Harrison."

Jake laughed. "Talk about ancient history."

"Do you still play football?"

"I switched to soccer when we moved to Cincinnati. Soccer's a spring sport, but I'm the extra point kicker for Hardy's football squad this season." He glanced over at her. "You coming to Friday night's game?"

"I'm planning to. Do you remember Rhonda? We're going together."

"You're the person I remember best," Jake said.

Dawn's heart tripped, and she could feel a blush creeping up her neck.

"Remember the school carnival?" Jake asked with a smile.

"Of course! You dressed up like a clown and sat in the dunk tank to help us cheerleaders raise money," she replied.

"I almost drowned."

"You were a life-saver." He groaned at her little joke. "Is this your car?" she asked.

"My parents got it for me when I turned sixteen this summer. It's not much, but it's mine."

She patted the worn seat. "I hope I can get a car when I turn sixteen."

He swung into the school parking lot, which was teeming with morning traffic. In the distance she saw school buses pulling in and was glad she hadn't had to ride one that morning. "Thanks for the lift," she said

24

when he'd found his assigned parking slot and turned off the engine.

"Maybe we can do it again." He walked with her toward the entrance and she couldn't help noticing that some of the girls were giving them curious looks.

"That would be fun." Because he was on the football team and because he was so good-looking, everybody would soon know who Jake Macka was, Dawn thought to herself. But this one morning, he was walking with her. In some ways, she felt like a thirteen-year-old again—like she had before she'd gotten cancer, when nothing was more important than being seen with one special person by all your friends.

"If you can hang around until I wrap up football practice, I'll take you home."

The urge to shout "Yes!" was on her tongue when she remembered that her mother was picking her up for a clinic appointment that afternoon. "I . . . um . . . can't today. I have someplace I have to go."

"Okay," he said.

She felt very disappointed. Once again, her stupid cancer had interfered with her life. If only she could be free of it forever. "It was really good to see you," she said, stopping beside her locker.

"You, too. I'd better go," he said. "I've got a bear for a geometry teacher. Rumor has it he gives detentions for tardies."

"Sounds mean."

He grinned, gave her a nod, and started off down the hall. She watched him disappear into the crowd and felt a bitter-sweet longing. Seeing Jake had stirred memories from a time when things were simple and life was uncomplicated. She sighed, wondering if life could ever be that way for her again.

*　*　*　*　*

"All finished?" Katie asked when Dawn walked up to her at the nurse's desk on the fourth floor.

"The bloodletting is over," Dawn replied, holding out her arm to show off the Snoopy Band-Aid in the crook of her elbow.

"Since I was a big girl and didn't cry, the lab tech gave me a special reward."

She and Katie laughed together. "I guess you get used to it after you've been through it as much as you have," Katie said.

Dawn shook her head. "Over the past three years, I'll bet they've withdrawn a small ocean of blood from me. Believe me,

I never get used to it!"

Katie flashed her a look of sympathy. "Well, when the report comes back and you're given a clean bill of health, you'll be glad."

"Until the next time. And speaking of that, I'll have to have a bone marrow aspiration next time." She made a face. "I hate when they stick needles into my bones. It hurts."

"But it's necessary," Katie said.

"I still hate it." Dawn shrugged. "So what do you want to show me?"

"It's upstairs."

"Not on the oncology floor, I hope," Dawn said. "You know how I feel about going back up there, Katie." She hated going to the cancer floor where she'd spent so much time in isolation when she'd almost died.

"It isn't." Katie took Dawn's hand.

They rode up to the tenth floor and stepped off the elevator. Dawn could see that it was a floor full of offices. Because it was after five, most of the workers had gone home. A few doctors were still inside their cubicles, doing paperwork or talking on the phone. A janitor was emptying wastebaskets.

"Have they given you your own office?" Dawn asked, intrigued.

Katie laughed. "No—I'm still only a nurse. Here we are," she said, turning a corner to face a long wall. On it, a tree was painted. The trunk was thick and sturdy looking, its branches sprawled down the wall as if it were actually growing there. Each branch held plump green leaves. Every leaf bore a person's name.

"What is it?" Dawn asked.

"It's the Tree of Life," Katie explained. "It's dedicated to cancer survivors. Like you, Dawn Rochelle."

Four

DAWN stepped forward and examined the painted tree more closely. Several of the large green leaves were only outlines, as if waiting for names to be filled in. "I don't understand," she said.

"It's a new program we've started," Katie said eagerly, her blue eyes sparkling with enthusiasm. "It's a survivor support group, and they meet right inside this room." She gestured toward a closed door beside the trunk of the tree. "All the members of the group have their names painted on the leaves to announce that they're survivors. Think of it, Dawn. Before bone marrow transplants came into being, less than a third of all kids with leukemia were cured. Today, more than half can expect a normal life span. Kids with other kinds of cancers are living longer too."

29

"That's great, but why have a support group? I mean, support groups are super when you've just been diagnosed. It really helps to be able to talk about treatments and feelings and stuff like that when it's happening to you. But if you're doing fine, why keep bringing it up?"

"Discussion groups are helpful no matter what the problem. And just because something's over doesn't mean it's one hundred percent behind you. Don't you ever wish that you could talk to someone who's been through what you've been through?" Katie asked.

Dawn wasn't sure how to answer. A part of her *was* curious about other cancer patients' experiences. But a part of her was also glad that much of the ordeal was behind her. She wasn't sure she wanted to dredge up the past and all its heartrending memories of treatments and pain and uncertainty.

Then there was the heartache of losing your friends to cancer. She'd worked long and hard to get over the feelings of loss she had when Sandy died. Then the feelings had all rushed back when she'd watched helplessly as Marlee died. What good would it do to discuss it with a bunch of strangers?

"I've just started high school and I'm pretty busy with my studies. I want to make good grades and be involved with school stuff. I'm not sure I'll have time to come to some support group." She stepped away from the mural of the tree.

"They only meet once a month. There are doctors and nurses who help guide the discussions and answer questions. A lot of kids your age attend. You might enjoy getting to know them."

"I hardly have time to get to know the kids at my school," Dawn said with a nervous laugh.

"You don't have to come regularly unless you want to." Katie put her hand on Dawn's arm. "There're a lot of things pent up inside you about your experiences. Things that need to be talked about."

"But I feel fine," Dawn protested, beginning to feel pressured. Why didn't Katie drop it?

"Do you?"

Katie's question added to Dawn's discomfort. Of course she did. Hadn't she faced her reluctance to be involved with other patients that summer when she agreed to be a counselor at the cancer camp? It had been hard to go back and perform the same

31

rituals she had during her very first summer. But she'd gone anyway and she ended up actually having a good time. "Look, Katie, I know you only want to help me, but right now I don't want to do anything that isn't connected with school. I want to have fun this year, you know, like a regular person."

"I understand. But will you just think about it? Just give it some thought?"

Dawn couldn't tell Katie no. She liked her too much. And she didn't want to hurt her feelings. But she didn't want to be forced into some cancer memory sessions either. "I'll think about it."

Katie smiled. "Good." She tucked her arm around Dawn's shoulders. "Now that that's settled, we'd better get you home. I'm starved for some of your mom's good cooking."

Dawn sneaked one final peek at the mural, at the leaves decorated with various names, and wished that Sandy's and Marlee's names could be listed.

But that was impossible. They weren't survivors. Sandy had leukemia, just like Dawn. Marlee had non-Hodgkins lymphoma, which causes tumors to grow on internal organs. Both had fought a tough battle with cancer, and both had lost. Dawn shook her head, trying to shake off the feeling of sadness that crept over her whenever she thought about Marlee and Sandy.

* * * * *

"Of course I remember Jake Macka! He was so cute! And he's here at Hardy? And he remembers you? Awesome!" Rhonda's voice bubbled. "Why didn't you *tell* me?"

"Calm down. It's not me he remembers. It's my cancer. I really didn't want to make a big deal of it."

Dawn and Rhonda were sitting in the stands. The football team had just jogged onto the field amid the cheers of the packed stadium.

"Where is he?" Rhonda craned her neck toward the field.

"That's him—number 6." Dawn had seen Jake instantly. It was as if her eyes had radar for him.

"Do you suppose he'll be at the dance?"

"How should I know?"

"You have all the luck," Rhonda grumbled. "First a college guy, and now Jake."

Dawn didn't remind Rhonda that her luck also included leukemia. "He was glad to see a familiar face. We had two years of information to catch up on, you know." Quickly, Dawn filled Rhonda in on what Jake had told her. "Once he gets popular at Hardy, he won't remember my name," she finished.

"We'll see," Rhonda declared.

After the game, Dawn and Rhonda shouldered their way through the crowd in the gym. "Let's grab a seat over there." Rhonda pointed to a section of bleachers reserved for general seating.

The center of the gym floor was jammed with dancers and a disc jockey was stationed at one end of the room. Colored spotlights reflected off the crowd. Music blared and Dawn had to shout to be heard. "Are we having fun yet?"

"Don't be a party pooper. We just got here." Rhonda grabbed Dawn's arm. "Maybe someone cool will notice us."

"Who? The janitor?" Even though she was giving Rhonda a hard time, Dawn was enjoying herself. She liked watching the dancers and feeling like she was part of things. The DJ announced "a blast from the past" and the mellow voice of Elvis Presley filled the gym. Couples glided together and swayed slowly to an old fifties love song.

The song jolted Dawn's memory, and suddenly she was back at camp, at the fifties dance with Brent. Brent had dressed as Elvis, and every female camper had flocked around him. She remembered walking in the moonlight with him, the feel of her hand in his. He'd pulled her into his arms and would have kissed her, but the girls from her cabin, hiding in the bushes, had begun heckling them.

All at once, she missed Brent terribly. She missed his easy and open personality and his low southern drawl. But what she missed most of all was the talks they'd had about Sandy. It had helped take away some of the pain of losing her.

"How about a dance?"

The voice above her jerked Dawn back to the present. But it wasn't Brent who was holding out his hand to her. It was Jake.

"She'd *love* to," Rhonda said, giving Dawn a shove.

Dawn was on her feet and in Jake's arms, still shaken by the powerful memories that had come upon her so unexpectedly. One minute she'd been having the time of her life, and the next, at the sound of a song, she'd dropped into a pit. What was wrong with her, anyway? "Great game," she said, trying to cheer herself up. "I'm glad we won."

"Thanks." His arms tightened around her. "Is everything all right?"

"Just fine." She offered him a breathless smile. His dark, chocolate brown eyes gazed down at her, and she felt an odd melting sensation going through her. *This is Jake!* she reminded herself. Someone she never thought she'd see again, and now, here they were dancing.

From the loudspeakers, Elvis's voice crooned, "Two different worlds, we live in two different worlds . . ." The words made perfect sense to her. Brent Chandler represented one of her worlds and Jake, another. Why did she feel as if she were caught between both of those worlds, but didn't fully belong to either?

Five

WHEN the song ended, Jake started to walk Dawn back to where Rhonda was sitting. Dawn tried to think of something clever to say—something to make him want to stick around awhile.

"Hey, Macka, wait up. I want to ask you something," a guy Dawn recognized as one of the senior players called out.

"Hi, Rich," Jake answered as the boy shouldered his way through the crowd toward them.

"We're going out for pizza and thought you might like to come along."

Jake glanced down at Dawn. "Gee, I don't know—"

"Go on," Dawn urged, not wanting him to feel obligated to her simply because they'd danced together.

A pretty girl with short dark hair

materialized beside Rich.

"This is my sister, Sharon," Rich said. Dawn recognized her as one of the Hardy cheerleaders.

"I've been wanting to meet you," Sharon said with a smile that flashed perfectly straight white teeth. "I thought you played an awesome game."

"Well, thanks." Jake smiled.

Dawn could tell that he was pleased by Sharon's attention.

Suddenly she felt like a third thumb. "I've got to run," she said.

"Are you sure?"

Dawn nodded. "Rhonda's waiting. It was great to see you again." She quickly made her way back to the bleachers, where Rhonda was tapping her toe impatiently. Dawn knew she wanted a full report.

"Let's go to the bathroom," Dawn said.

In the crowded bathroom, they found a small space next to a tiled wall. "I saw the whole thing," Rhonda announced. "Who does that girl think she is? Barging in on you like that."

"She's one of the most popular girls in this school and she can do anything she wants." Dawn's heart was pounding.

"Well, you didn't have to give up so

38

easily," Rhonda insisted. "You were there first. Jake asked you to dance, not her."

"He wanted to go with them. I could tell."

"You didn't give him any other choice." Rhonda eyed her. "What's wrong with you, anyway? You get offered a great opportunity and you run away. Jake Macka is so cool. I don't get it, Dawn. What's your problem?"

Dawn had no answer. She couldn't put her problem into words because she couldn't understand it herself. She wanted to have fun and act normal, but something was holding her back. "My problem is that I want to go home," she told Rhonda. "I'm sorry I'm such a drag, but I don't want to hang around any more tonight. I'm going to call my dad to come pick me up. If you want to stay, it's all right."

"I don't want to stay if you don't," Rhonda said limply. Dawn started for the door, but Rhonda caught her arm. "It's okay this time," she said, "but please don't be like this next time we come to a dance. How're we ever going to get noticed, if we never hang around?"

*   *   *   *   *

In October, Rob came home for a weekend.

"Hey Squirt," he said, giving her a hug. He pulled back and looked her over. "I guess I can't call you that anymore."

"That's right. I've added a half-inch to the four I grew over the summer." Dawn's chemo and radiation treatments had stunted her growth. It had taken her longer to mature in every way. All the previous year she'd felt extremely self-conscious about her lack of curves, but now, with Rob's bone marrow working and her drug therapies greatly reduced, she was finally growing and developing again.

"So I'll have to come up with a new nickname." Rob puckered his brow. "How about 'hotshot'? You *are* taking Hardy High by storm, aren't you?"

"Not quite. There's over a thousand students at Hardy. I'm afraid I'm just a speck on the wall."

"Not for long, I'll bet."

Dawn wished she shared his confidence in her, but she felt so ordinary. And except for Jake, who was busy with football, classes, and Sharon's attentions, she didn't see much excitement coming her way.

The phone rang and her mother called, "Dawn, it's for you."

She decided to take it in her room. "Don't

be too long," Rob said as she started up the stairs. "I have an important call to make."

"Really? Anybody I know?" she teased over her shoulder, knowing full well it was Katie.

"Just don't gab all afternoon."

She was still laughing when she picked up the receiver in her room.

"Got time for an old friend?" Brent Chandler asked.

Both surprised and pleased to hear his voice, she sprawled across her bed eagerly. "Brent! How are you?"

"I'm fine. And I've been thinking a lot about you lately."

"I thought college life was supposed to be exciting."

"Well, it is. But it's hard too," he confessed. "I've missed everybody. My family. Friends. I've been thinking a lot about camp this past summer. And all the great times you and I had."

She couldn't deny that being with him had made her time as a counselor extra special. "I thought you would have forgotten all about me by now."

"No way."

Goose bumps skittered up her arms. "I've missed you too," she said quietly.

"I was hoping you'd say that."

"Why?"

"I want to come see you over Christmas break."

Her heart skipped a beat. "You do?"

"Don't sound so surprised." His laugh warmed her. "I know it's a bit early to be making plans, but we have a long break, and I'd really like to see you. I was thinking of coming a week before Christmas, staying a couple of days, then heading home in time to spend the holidays with the folks. What do you think? Would your parents mind?"

Dawn knew that Sandy's brother would be welcome anytime. "I'm sure it won't be a problem," she said. "We have a spare bedroom in our basement. I'll ask and write you."

"Good. I'll be looking for your letter." She heard someone in the background yell for Brent to get off the phone. "Bye for now," he said.

She hung up, but the sound of his soft southern voice lingered in her head. She could barely contain her excitement. Brent wanted to come see her! She wanted to see him too—very much. She bolted to the door and took the stairs two at a time. She needed to talk to her mother. And then she had to tell Rhonda.

"Mom!" Dawn bounded into the kitchen only to see her mother, Rob, and Katie standing together in a huddle. She skidded to a stop. "Katie, you're here! I didn't know—" The words died on her lips as she glanced from face to face. "Something's wrong," Dawn said. "I can tell. What is it?"

"Oh, honey," Katie said, stepping forward from the group and taking both of Dawn's hands. Katie's big blue eyes looked troubled. "I came straight from the hospital because I wanted to tell you the bad news myself."

"What bad news?" Dawn's heart pounded and a queasy sensation filled her stomach.

"Mrs. Hodges, Marlee's grandmother, died this morning."

Six

THE October air felt crisp and cool. The thick green grass was clipped and neat, as orderly as the rows of bronze plaques and flower-laden vases that stretched as far as Dawn could see in the immaculate cemetery. It was the last place she wanted to be on a Saturday afternoon. But when her parents and Katie and Rob had said they should all go to Mrs. Hodges's funeral, she couldn't think of a way to get out of it.

The minister spoke highly of Mrs. Hodges and of her wonderful contributions to their community. Across from her, Dawn recognized the mayor, and she realized how important Mrs. Hodges must have been. Beside him stood Mrs. Hodges's attorney. He had surprised Dawn by knowing her name. "So, you're Miss Rochelle," he'd said. "Mrs. Hodges thought very highly of you."

Dawn swallowed hard, trying not to cry. Mrs. Hodges was very old and had been sick with a heart condition for a long time. She'd practically raised her granddaughter, Marlee, showering her with wonderful things. The two of them had lived in a mansion, and Marlee had been the only one at summer camp with designer sheets and a limo for transportation. But even though Mrs. Hodges could give Marlee anything money could buy, she couldn't make her cancer go away.

". . . ashes to ashes, dust to dust," the minister said.

Dawn kept remembering Marlee's funeral and how Mrs. Hodges had given her back her worn-out teddy bear, Mr. Ruggers, along with a farewell note from Marlee. At least now Marlee and her grandmother were both in heaven together. She tried to comfort herself with that thought.

"Hey Squirt, it's over." Rob's voice startled Dawn out of her thoughts.

Dawn glanced around and saw that people were beginning to disperse or gather in small groups. Her parents were talking to the minister, and Katie was talking to a fellow nurse. "Tell Mom I'll be waiting in

45

the car," she said, struggling to hold back tears. She began walking toward their car, parked in a long line of cars from the funeral procession. More than anything, she just wanted to go home and forget all the sadness.

She was almost to the car when she heard a familiar voice.

"Dawn?"

Jake's voice so unnerved her that she dropped her purse on the ground. He stooped to pick it up.

"What are you doing here?" she asked in shrill voice. Although she was standing in wide open space, she felt cornered and trapped. Jake wasn't supposed to be part of this world, and his presence felt like an intrusion.

"I work here some weekends. I help with grounds maintenance," he explained. "You all right?"

"I'm fine," she lied, wanting him to go away and leave her alone. Her emotions were on a roller coaster, and she couldn't trust herself not to burst into tears in front of him.

"Did you . . ." Jake's voice caught a little. He started again, "Did you lose someone close to you?"

"No one. I mean, friend. Sort of . . ." she stumbled. Jake smiled a kind smile, but Dawn could tell he was confused by her response. She took a deep breath, forcing her racing heart to slow its pace. "It was the grandmother of a friend. A girl I knew."

"Knew?"

Dawn winced, hating her slip of the tongue. "It doesn't matter. They're both dead now."

"Listen, if you'd like to talk about it—"

"I don't! I don't want to even think about it. I just want to go home!"

Jake took a step backward, as if she'd shoved him. "Dawn, I'm sorry," he said softly.

Dawn felt tears brimming in her eyes. She was embarrassed by her outburst, but didn't know how to make him understand. She *had* to get away! She didn't want Jake to see her cry. She didn't want him feeling any sorrier for her than he already did. Without another word, she turned and jogged to the car. Once inside, she buried her face in her hands and sobbed.

* * * * *

"Come on, Dawn. It'll be fun." As they walked home from the bus stop on Monday,

47

Rhonda was urging Dawn to join her on the Hardy High Christmas Dance committee. "We can help with the decorations. It'll be a good way to meet some people—maybe even some cute guys."

"Don't you ever give up?"

Actually, helping out on the dance sounded like good idea to Dawn. It would give her something to think about besides the awful way she'd treated Jake on Saturday. She felt so embarrassed, she could hardly look at him in the hall. How was she ever going to apologize? He probably thought she was nuts.

"So I'll tell the head of the dance committee we'll be at the meeting," Rhonda said cheerfully. "This is going to be just like old times. Remember in eighth grade when we did stuff like this together?"

Dawn couldn't believe it had been that long since she'd participated in a school project with Rhonda. Yet, when she thought back, all she could recall were days and nights in the hospital or stuck in bed at home because her medications had made her so sick.

"I have lots to catch up on," she told Rhonda. "Maybe this is a good place to start."

On Friday, small group of kids gathered in the gym to plan the dance. Dawn recognized several cheerleaders, including Sharon Lewis, who constantly hung around Jake.

They voted to call the dance "The Snowflake Ball" and to decorate with giant, glittery snowflake cut-outs that would dangle from the gym ceiling. One of the girls announced, "My grandfather has an old-fashioned sleigh. We could put it in a corner and drape it with angel hair and fake snow. I think it would add atmosphere." They all agreed.

Dawn's brain was buzzing with suggestions, and she busily wrote them down for when they broke into smaller groups. As she was dragging her chair to the area where the decorations committee would meet, she noticed Sharon staring at her, as if she wanted to speak to her. Sucking up her breath, Dawn asked, "Is something wrong?"

"No, nothing," Sharon said quickly, but Dawn could tell something was definitely on the girl's mind.

"Are you sure?"

"Well, I do want to ask you something," Sharon confessed.

"What's that?" Dawn tried to look friendly, but somehow she just didn't trust Sharon.

Sharon glanced at the two cheerleaders who had walked up to stand next to her. "I hope you won't think this is too personal," Sharon began. "But I'm just dying of curiosity. Is that your real hair? Or is it a wig?"

Seven

CAUGHT off guard by the bluntness of Sharon's question, Dawn fingered her hair self-consciously.

"Your hair—is it real?" Sharon's face was the picture of innocence, but Dawn suspected her motives weren't innocent. "I was told you have cancer, and I thought people with cancer go bald, and so I was just wondering about your hair. If it's a wig, it looks real. If it isn't, then how come it didn't fall out?"

Dawn felt her cheeks flame red. But she held her head high, determined not to let Sharon get under her skin. "This is my 'real' hair. Sometimes chemotherapy makes hair fall out, but not always. Even if it does, the hair grows back."

"But you *do* have cancer?" Sharon queried.

The other two girls were watching closely, and Dawn wasn't sure how to answer. Saying yes would give Sharon some kind of perverse pleasure, but Dawn couldn't lie. She felt an urge to bolt for the door, but she didn't want to give Sharon the satisfaction. "I'm being treated for a form of leukemia," Dawn finally replied quietly. "I'm in remission and have been for well over a year."

"I was just curious," Sharon declared. "I've never known anyone with cancer before."

Dawn calmly headed toward her small group. She didn't look back, even when one of Sharon's friends said, "Honestly, Sharon, that was so totally rude of you."

"What's rude?" she heard Sharon ask innocently. "Can't a person ask a question around here?"

Dawn had lost her enthusiasm for the dance committee. She looked for Rhonda, but Rhonda was with a boy, staring raptly up at his face, hanging on his every word.

She scooped up her books and walked out the door. Once she was outside, her hands began to shake and her knees quivered. Hot tears rushed to her eyes. Now that Sharon knew about her cancer, all of

Hardy High would know. And she'd acted so hateful about it—as if cancer had been something Dawn had contracted to gain attention. Was this disease going to follow her everywhere for the rest of her life?

* * * * * *

"Why'd you run off? Good grief, Dawn, you were there one minute and the next time I looked around, you were nowhere. Where'd you go?"

Dawn listened patiently on the phone while Rhonda fussed at her. "I remembered something I had to do," she replied.

"You could have told me."

"You were busy talking with some guy."

"You could have interrupted. *I* would have if I had to run off. I asked everybody where you'd gone, but no one knew anything. It was like you evaporated into thin air."

"Well, if you must know, I got blindsided by Sharon Lewis," Dawn confessed. Switching the receiver to her other ear, she quickly told Rhonda about her run-in with Sharon.

"What a cat. She's just jealous," Rhonda declared after hearing the story.

"Jealous? Of me? Get real! Why should she be?"

"Because she can't keep Jake Macka's undivided attention."

The thought of Jake reminded her of how she treated him at the cemetery. "That's hard to believe. Maybe Jake really likes her."

"Not by a long shot. The word is he's nobody's property. And that Sharon's making a pest of herself."

"How do you know these things?"

"I keep my ear to the ground."

The image of Rhonda down on all fours in a Hardy hallway with her ear plastered to the floor made Dawn giggle. "Don't get run over," she joked.

"And don't *you* run away every time someone like Sharon acts like an idiot."

"You don't understand," Dawn started.

"Then explain it to me."

Dawn knew that she couldn't. Sandy had understood completely. But Rhonda—well, Rhonda just wasn't Sandy.

"I mean, you can't get all bent out of shape whenever someone asks you about it." Rhonda made it sound as if Dawn should put off the past like one would take off a jacket.

"Rhonda, I actually died and got resuscitated. That sort of thing makes an impact on a person."

"You make it sound as if I should apologize for not having shared the experience. As if I missed out on something."

Rhonda's remark stabbed at Dawn. It made her feel much the same as Sharon's remarks had—like cancer was something she'd chosen in order to gain attention. She twisted the cord around her finger. "You missed a lot of pain. I wouldn't wish what I went through on my worst enemy. And I don't mean just having cancer. Do you know what it's like to have your best friend die?"

A long silence stretched between them. Dawn stared at the light from her bedside table lamp, reflecting off the wall. Beyond the puddle of light, shadows loomed. Rhonda broke the tension with, "I know what it's like to be afraid my best friend *would* die. I told you a long time ago that I was sorry about Sandy. I didn't know her, but I know how much you liked her."

Rhonda sounded hurt, which made Dawn feel bad for even bringing Sandy into the conversation. "Rhonda, this discussion is going no place. Why don't we just drop it?

I'm sorry I took off this afternoon without saying anything to you. I'm sorry I let Sharon get to me. I'll try not to let it happen again."

"Sure," Rhonda said. "Let's just forget the whole thing."

"So, when's the next committee meeting?"

"Monday. Does that mean you'll be back?"

"I'll be back." Dawn meant it, too. Sharon Lewis wasn't going to keep her away. And although she didn't like the idea of kids at Hardy knowing about her cancer, there wasn't anything she could do about it. It was a part of her life and nothing could make it go away.

* * * * *

By Thanksgiving week, plans for the dance were well underway, and Dawn and Rhonda had worked hard at cutting out hundreds of oversized snowflakes. Dawn stayed clear of Sharon, who let it be known that *she* was going to the dance with Jake. Dawn tried not to let it bother her. Jake was polite to her, acting as if the scene at the cemetery had never happened, yet he didn't attempt to call her or offer her rides to school.

56

"Don't be greedy," Rhonda told her. "You've got Brent coming to visit, and he seems much more interested in you than Jake does." Rhonda was right, of course. Dawn really was looking forward to Brent's visit, but still she couldn't control the funny way her heart beat every time she saw Jake in the halls.

The day before Thanksgiving, Dawn was in the kitchen helping her mother get a headstart on the holiday meal when the phone rang. Rob, home for the weekend, grabbed the receiver, then offered it to Dawn. "It's Katie and she says she needs to talk to you. Right now."

Surprised, Dawn took the phone. "Hi. What's up?"

"What are you doing Friday?" Katie's voice sounded excited.

"Hitting the mall bright and early with Rhonda to start Christmas shopping."

"Wrong," Katie replied. "You're coming with me to a special meeting of the hospital board. The administrator is making a big announcement, and he wants *you* to be there."

Eight

"**D**O I look all right? Is my hair messed up?" Dawn asked. She sat in the waiting area of the offices of Dr. Marcus Douglas, Executive Director of the Columbus hospital, where she'd spent so much of her last three years undergoing cancer treatments. Both Katie and her mother were with her.

"You look fine," Katie assured her. "Very pretty in that shade of green."

Dawn smoothed the skirt of her best dress. "Couldn't you find out what this is all about?"

Katie shook her head. "Every floor of the hospital is buzzing with some kind of theory, but no one knows anything definite."

"I'm sure it's something exciting," her mother added. Dawn couldn't imagine why she'd been summoned, and no amount of thinking or talking about it had turned up any possibilities. What could the hospital possibly want with her?

Just then the outer office door opened. A cameraman from a local TV news station stepped inside. Another man and two women, apparently reporters, followed. Dr. Douglas's secretary stepped forward, offering the guests a broad smile. "Welcome. I'll tell Dr. Douglas that all of you have arrived."

Moments later, the inner office door swung open and several distinguished looking men emerged. A round of introductions was made. The mayor was there, as well as several other politicians and hospital department heads. A man with a thick head of silver hair stepped up to her and held out his hand. "Hello, Dawn. Remember me? Franklin Chase. We met at Mrs. Hodges's funeral service. I'm her attorney and I'm handling her estate."

Dawn smiled and shook his hand. Dr. Douglas ushered the entire troop into his spacious office. Sunlight flooded the room through banks of windows along one side. At one end of the room, a table held a scaled-down model of the hospital. "This way," Dr. Douglas said, and he led the way to the model.

Dawn crowded around the table with the rest of the guests and studied the model, fascinated. It reminded her of an elaborate dollhouse, complete with miniature shrubs, lampposts, and parking lots. Then, off to one side of the model, she saw a sleek, modern-looking addition.

Dr. Douglas said, "It gives me great pleasure to announce that, thanks to the generosity of a benefactor, we will build the Marlee Hodges Cancer Treatment Center."

When the applause died down, Dawn could hear the TV camera whirl. A film of tears filled her eyes as emotion swept through her. So that was what Mrs. Hodges did with her money—she funded a much-needed treatment center in honor of her granddaughter. She had wanted so badly for Marlee to be cured, and though Marlee couldn't be cured, she had dedicated her wealth to a center for other cancer patients in the hope that they could.

Dawn felt her mother's hand slip into hers and squeeze.

"That's right," Mr. Chase, the attorney, added. "It was Amanda's wish that a special unit be built and dedicated to Marlee—a unit to treat even more kids with cancer."

"We definitely need the space," Dr. Douglas said. "This addition will give us a hundred more beds and several outpatient areas, as well as the newest, most technologically advanced equipment available to treat all forms of cancer in children."

"When will it be opened?" one of the reporters asked.

"We'll break ground on Easter weekend. The facility should take about eighteen months to complete."

Dawn hardly heard other questions. She kept gazing down at the scale model, thinking about Marlee. Marlee was such a puzzle. She had wanted so much to be part of the gang, yet she was so aloof—sometimes downright mean. She would probably have had something smart-aleck to say about the whole project. But Dawn knew that Marlee would have been very pleased; the smart remarks would have been her way of covering up her pleasure.

". . . Dawn Rochelle." At the sound of her name, Dawn startled. Mr. Chase was smiling and everyone was looking at her, including the man with the TV camera. "Dawn, I know you must be very curious as to why you were invited today."

"Yes, sir," she said, feeling her heartbeat

accelerate.

"It was Amanda Hodges's wish that you say a few words at the groundbreaking ceremony."

Dawn swallowed hard. Her? Say something with a bunch of important people watching? She was thinking of a way to get out of it when Mr. Chase added, "More than that, she also wanted you to help gather artifacts that will be placed in a special box. This box will be sealed and buried beside the building's cornerstone and will act as a kind of time capsule. It won't be opened for one hundred years."

An excited buzz went through the room. *A hundred years!* "But—but what will I put in it?"

"That will be left entirely to your discretion. Mrs. Hodges felt that when it is opened, people from the twenty-first century should have a glimpse of what was important to young cancer victims of today. She wanted you in charge of the project, Dawn, because of your kindness to Marlee and because of your own fight against leukemia."

Dawn was speechless. She didn't know what to think. For one thing, she certainly didn't feel qualified for such an important task—she didn't want to be responsible for selecting the items to be sealed inside some time capsule. And for another, she wanted to forget about her cancer, not be reminded of it. Frantically, she searched for a way to beg off. Then she saw her mother's face, glowing with pride. And Katie's, beaming with pleasure.

Dawn's objections died on her lips. Against her will, she heard herself say, "I'll do it." A flash went off in her face and several of the dignitaries stepped closer to her. Her head was swimming, her stomach tied in knots, but she managed a smile for the hard round eye of the TV camera.

Later, when the interviews were over and the pictures had all been taken, Dawn, her mother, and Katie retreated to the hospital coffee shop. "Oh, Dawn, I'm so proud of you!" her mother gushed.

"What will I say? What will I put in the time capsule?"

"You've got five months to think about it," Katie replied. "I'm sure you'll come up with something that's absolutely perfect."

Five months didn't seem long enough. Five *years* hardly seemed time enough.

"Mrs. Hodges wouldn't have selected you if she hadn't been confident of your ability,"

Dawn's mother said, scooting away from the table to get another cup of coffee.

Once she had walked to the coffee urn, Katie gazed at Dawn with a thoughtful expression. "What is it?" Dawn asked.

"I was just wondering if you ever gave any more thought to coming to the survivor support group I told you about."

Immediately, the sprawling tree with painted leaves along the corridor wall sprang to Dawn's mind. She glanced down at the half-empty cup of hot chocolate. "I've been busy."

"Perhaps meeting with some of these people, others like yourself, could give you some ideas for your project. I know for a fact that they're meeting three weeks from today—"

"Oh, I can't. That's the night of the big Christmas dance."

Katie looked disappointed, but brightened and asked, "Are you going with anyone special?"

"No. Rhonda and I volunteered to help the photographer. We have a sled all decorated with bells and artificial snow. We think it'll make a good backdrop for memory photos." She didn't add that Jake would have been the only boy she'd have

64

wanted to go with, and he was taking Sharon.

"There's another meeting after New Year's," Katie suggested. "How about coming in January?"

"Maybe," Dawn said evasively. "I'll see. I mean, who knows what the New Year will bring?" But privately she knew why she wasn't giving a straight answer about attending the meetings. It was more than putting the past behind her. It was more than not wanting to hash over her past experiences with cancer, to dredge up old memories, and mourn the loss of old friends. Deep down, inside the deepest part of her heart, in spite of all the encouraging lab reports from her doctors, she wasn't a hundred percent sure she could call herself a survivor and a winner. With the ongoing tests and medications and the possibility of a relapse, she simply wasn't *sure*.

Nine

"DOESN'T everything look wonderful?" Dawn asked Rhonda as they stood together in the gym.

"It's hard to believe we were still running around hanging snowflakes and icicles at four this afternoon," Rhonda said with a chuckle. "Looking at you now, one would never know."

Surprised, Dawn looked down at herself. The dress she wore belonged to Katie. It was an incandescent green color that shimmered in the dim light. She'd worn her hair long, clipped back on one side with a green bow. With Rhonda standing next to her in a brilliant red dress, Dawn thought they complemented each other quite well.

The gym looked like a winter wonderland. At the main entrance, twin igloos stood on either side of the doorway. Tables, draped in white paper cloths and adorned with centerpieces of styrofoam snowmen, ringed the dance floor. The refreshment table was heaped with frosted Christmas cookies, chocolate brownies, bowls of red punch, and a large frosted gingerbread house. Lights had been lowered and colored candles glimmered from every table. A mirrored ball spun overhead, reflecting light on the dancers below.

"I wish I were with someone special," Rhonda said with a sigh.

"There's always next year," Dawn told her, determined not to let Rhonda start feeling sorry for herself because she didn't have a boyfriend. "Come on. The photographer's setting up his gear."

They wove their way around the tables where groups of kids sat, all decked out in satin, lace, and suits. Dawn forced herself not to look for Jake and Sharon. She didn't want to start feeling sorry for *herself* either.

The photographer gave them each a task. It was Dawn's responsibility to make certain that names and addresses were correct on cards of couples wanting photos of themselves, and that each card was filed to coincide with the correct frame of exposed film.

The sleigh looked picture-perfect with its leather bench seat and dark wood sides. The runners were decorated with tiny twinkling lights. It all looked so inviting that couples began to line up early for photographs. Dawn went to work and in no time was completely involved in her job.

She began to notice that many kids spoke to her by name, which surprised her. If she hadn't been so busy, she might have tried to figure it out, but the line for photos kept growing longer, and she found herself taking information as fast as she could write.

"Macka," a boy's voice said, above her shoulder. "Jake Macka. Hi, Dawn."

Dawn almost dropped the pencil. Jake wore a charcoal-gray suit and white shirt, set off by a red silk tie. He was smiling, but Dawn couldn't shake the image of the hurt expression she'd seen on his face at the cemetery.

"And Sharon Lewis," Sharon cooed from beside him. Sharon was dressed in pure white. Her hair sparkled with gold glitter but was stiff with hairspray. Her smile seemed forced and a little too perfect.

"Proofs will be mailed in two weeks," Dawn said as she wrote their names on the cards. She handed them each a form to give to the photographer and tried to look the other way when they stood together in front of the sleigh, arms around one another for the camera.

Once the photo was taken, Jake and Sharon stepped out of the bright lights. Dawn resolved to ignore them and the crazy way her heart was thudding. From the corner of her eye, she saw Rhonda approaching, carrying two cups of punch. Somehow, when Rhonda was directly in front of Sharon, she tripped and spilled bright red liquid all over the bottom of Sharon's dress.

"You idiot!" Sharon cried. "Look at what you did!"

Rhonda gasped, set the cups down on the registration table, and exclaimed, "Oh, goodness! Klutzy me. I'm *so* sorry." She hastily tried to wipe off the dress with a blank registration card.

"Get away from me," Sharon demanded, shaking the soggy, stained hem of her dress while glaring at Rhonda.

"You should wash it off right away," a helpful bystander offered.

Sharon's face was the color of the punch as she told Jake, "I'm going to try to undo some of this damage. Wait for me at our table."

Dawn thought she sounded awfully bossy. "I'll hang around," Jake mumbled, and Dawn could have sworn he was attempting not to laugh out loud over the incident.

Rhonda fanned herself with the crumpled card as they all watched Sharon stalk off in a huff. "It was an accident," Rhonda said, her eyes all wide with innocence. "She didn't have to bite my head off."

Dawn knew she saw mischief in Rhonda's eyes and vowed to ask her later whether it was really an accident. Rhonda hauled Dawn out of the chair. "Take a break," she said. "Let me do this for a while." She held up the empty cup. "Maybe you'd better get us another drink. I'm positively parched."

Jake took Dawn's arm. "Come on, I'll walk you over to the refreshment table." They were skirting the edge of the dance floor when Jake stopped and said, "Let's dance."

"But I should get back."

"Rhonda's handling things. You can take time for one dance." He put his arms around her. "You look lovely tonight," he said. "And your hair looks so soft."

Dawn was glad she hadn't weighted it down with hairspray, so it still looked and felt soft and natural. "I'm really sorry about Sharon's dress," she said.

"I'm really sorry about Sharon."

"What do you mean?"

"Look, Dawn—I didn't *want* to come with her. I sort of . . ." Jake studied his toes. "Well, I sort of got tricked into it. I'm sorry."

Dawn took a deep breath and added, "And I'm really sorry about that afternoon at the cemetery, too."

"Ancient history," he said. "I forgot all about it.

He might have forgotten, but she hadn't. "I felt bad about the way I acted. I should have said something before now, but . . ." she let the sentence trail off, embarrassed and tongue-tied.

"I know about your friendship with Marlee."

"You do? How?"

"Rhonda." He gestured toward the photo table. "I cornered her and talked her into telling me."

"She never said a word to me." Dawn was shocked and a little angry, too. She knew what a gossip Rhonda could be. She hated knowing that Rhonda and Jake had discussed her and her private feelings.

"Please don't be mad at Rhonda," Jake said, as if sensing how she felt. "I would have rather have heard the story from you, but you were so upset at the funeral, I wasn't sure how to bring it up again."

Dawn's anger passed, but she wasn't sure what to say next. Jake must have sensed how she was feeling. He held her a little closer and said, "That was a pretty cool article about you in the newspaper. My mom said you were on TV, too, but I didn't see it."

"Well, it wasn't really about me. It was about the new cancer wing of the hospital."

"All I know is that Mom showed me the paper and there you were on the front page. Everyone in school saw it, too."

That explains why everyone acts like they know me, Dawn told herself. "Well I'd rather be in the paper because I did something great," Dawn told him. "Like kicking the field goal that put Hardy into the state play-offs."

"And missing the one that knocked us out of the championship," Jake added ruefully. "So what are you going to say at the ground-breaking ceremony?"

"I only wish I knew." Dawn noticed that the music had ended, but Jake was still holding her close. "I guess it'll be like a term paper—I'll figure it out the night before it's due."

He laughed, making her feel clever. "You have a busy Christmas break planned?" he asked.

She couldn't tell him about Brent coming, and didn't want to mention her upcoming appointment for a day-long visit to the clinic. "My brother's graduating early from Michigan State and my family's going up for the ceremony. How about you?"

"My family's going out to visit my grandparents. We'll be gone until New Year's Day."

She felt the keen edge of disappointment and told herself she was being silly. She couldn't wait to see Brent, couldn't wait to talk to him, spend time with him. So why did her emotions get so confused whenever she was with Jake? "I'd better get that punch before Rhonda sends out a search party," she said.

Jake walked her to the refreshment table, picked up a full cup, then walked her back to the table where Rhonda was happily writing names and flirting with every

73

cute guy. "It's about time," said Rhonda. "I thought the two of you had been kidnapped." She gave Dawn a sly wink.

"We wanted to make sure we didn't trip and spill any on the way." Dawn turned to face Jake. "So, I guess I'll see you in January."

"I guess so." Jake caught her hand. "Have a great Christmas, Dawn."

"You too, Jake." Dawn watched him walk away, feeling a letdown she couldn't explain.

Ten

ROB Rochelle graduated from Michigan State University on the third Saturday in December in a ceremony held on the campus. Dawn sat with her parents and Katie in the stands, watching with awe and a sense of pride. The University Chancellor, dressed in the distinctive dark robe and colored hood that designated his academic position, led the dignified procession of professors, graduates, and baccalaureate students. Stately music played over the sound system while Dawn's gaze followed the long line of black graduation caps down the aisles to the front of the auditorium.

Because Rob had told them his approximate location, Dawn was able to pick him out in the steady stream of bobbing flat black hats and dangling green-and-white tassels. A lump rose to her throat as she watched him. *Rob, my big brother.* Without him and his gift of bone marrow, she would certainly be dead.

Hi, Squirt. His pet name rang in her ears. His was the first face she remembered seeing when the doctors had resuscitated her. He had looked ghastly pale and terrified. She would remember the look always, because she'd never seen him look that scared before. She hoped she never had to see such an expression on his face again.

Her mother reached over and squeezed Dawn's hand as Rob's name was called. Dawn held her breath as he crossed the stage, took the offered diploma, shook the Chancellor's hand, and walked back to his seat. From the corner of her eye, she saw her mother dabbing her eyes with a tissue and her father smiling broadly.

She knew that she had a long way to go before she would get a college diploma. *Besides, you don't even know what you want to study*, she reminded herself. A shadow of doubt flickered across her mind. *Will I even be alive?* Would Rob's bone marrow continue to function? Was her battle with cancer truly over? Dawn refused to speculate. Anything could happen in the next few years.

"Wasn't it fabulous?" Katie asked when the ceremony was complete. They were waiting in the crowded lobby for Rob to find them.

"I can't believe my baby boy's all grown up." Dawn's mother sighed.

"Mom, he's hardly a baby."

"You'll both always be my babies," she insisted.

Dawn watched the crowds surging around them. Suddenly, she caught sight of a small blond woman posing for photographs nearby. She jabbed Katie in the ribs. "That's her! There's Darcy Collin, the girl Rob used to be engaged to."

Katie's eyes narrowed as she studied Darcy. "She sure is pretty," Katie said. "No wonder Rob fell in love with her."

"Looks aren't everything," Dawn reminded her, wanting to find a way to make her feel better. "She's not half as nice as you are."

"I remember when Rob and Darcy broke their engagement. You were in isolation, fighting for your life when it happened. He was awfully depressed."

"He told me how you talked to him. And you've helped him get over her totally," Dawn replied with a confident smile. "You

77

have nothing to worry about."

"I really care for Rob." Katie cast a long glance toward Darcy who was talking excitedly with several people. "But when I see how pretty she is . . ."

Dawn immediately thought about Sharon. "Why do we always feel inferior whenever a prettier girl comes around a guy we like?"

Katie arched her brow. "Is there somebody in your life you've never mentioned to me?"

"Not exactly. I mean there's a guy at school who makes me crazy sometimes. But then Brent's coming next week and I know I like him. And—and—" she threw up her hands in frustration. "I don't know what to think. How can I like two guys at the same time?"

"It isn't hard," Katie said with a laugh. "You're lucky you have choices. Tell me about the boy at school."

Dawn wished she'd never brought it up. The crowds around them were beginning to thin out, and she didn't want her parents overhearing her. She saw that they were in a conversation with several other parents. Hesitantly, she said, "His name's Jake, and I've known him since fifth grade. I had a crush on him. You know—elementary school stuff. But I've been through so much these past few years, he could never understand. Brent does, though, because he went through it with Sandy, and he was a counselor at camp. I like the comfortable way he makes me feel."

"Have you ever given Jake a chance to understand?"

"I don't know how to talk to him about it. It's like I have two separate lives. One of me has been through all this stuff with cancer. The other me is just a regular person who's almost sixteen and trying to get on with her life. It's hard being in two worlds at once. I . . . I'm not sure I want to involve Jake in the cancer world."

"Maybe that's a choice he should make."

Dawn was uncomfortable with the discussion. It was difficult to put her doubts and feelings into words. "It probably won't matter anyway. I think he might like somebody else."

Katie gave Dawn a compassionate look. "You know, before I met Rob, I was dating a guy pretty seriously."

"You were?"

"Tony and I were a steady item. I even thought about marrying him."

"Do you still like him?"

"I'll always *like* him." She put her hand on Dawn's arm. "He's a wonderful friend. But I don't love him."

Rob had thought he was in love with Darcy, but their love hadn't worked out. Dawn found it all very confusing. "How do you know whether you're in love with somebody or not?"

"It sounds corny, but you just *know*." Katie offered a smile. "Love isn't *only* body chemistry, you know. It's a lot of other things."

"So what should I look for?"

"I'm hardly an expert," Katie said with a laugh. "But I do know that love is patient and trusting; it doesn't hold a grudge when somebody hurts you, and most of all, it endures. The Bible says that love is greater than even faith and hope. That sounds pretty big to me."

"I wonder if I'll ever find it. And if I do, I wonder if I'll recognize it."

"You have plenty of other things to do first," Katie said. "You have school to finish and a career to plan. I think you even have to get your driver's license first."

Dawn burst out laughing. "I guess you're right. I don't have to settle on anyone right now." She glanced toward Darcy, who was walking off with a good-looking dark haired man. "And you don't have a thing to worry about. You're the one Rob thinks about, talks about, probably dreams about."

"I'd better be," Katie said with a grin. "I know he's the one I think about."

*　*　*　*　*

Dawn fidgeted with the curtain at the living room window and peered out into the cold darkness. She'd been anticipating Brent's arrival all day. He'd called around suppertime to say he was about an hour away. She glanced at the mantel clock and wondered why time seemed to be moving so slowly.

Behind her, the Christmas tree twinkled and glittered with decorations. A few packages lay underneath, including the one with the thick, cable-knit sweater she'd bought for Brent. The scent of bayberry and evergreen hung in the room and Christmas music played softly on the CD player.

She was more nervous than she'd ever imagined she'd be. She hadn't seen Brent since June, when camp ended. They had stood together on a cabin porch, watching

81

the rain pouring down, and he'd taken her in his arms and kissed her. She could still recall the soft feel of his lips on hers.

A bright beam of headlights swept across Dawn's face, startling her. Out the window, she saw a car in her driveway. Her heart thudded in renewed anticipation—Brent Chandler had arrived.

Eleven

DAWN waited for Brent to ring the doorbell. She didn't want to seem too anxious, after all. When she opened the door, the icy December air rushed inside, but she hardly felt it. Brent was dressed in jeans and a leather jacket. His blond hair spilled low on his forehead and his slow, easy grin warmed her. For a moment they stood looking at one another.

"Don't I even get a hug?" Brent drawled.

She threw herself into his arms. "I'm so glad you're here!" She pulled him into the coziness of the living room. "Are you all right? Did you have a good trip? Do you want a soda?"

"Whoa," he said with a laugh. "One thing at a time. "Yes, yes, and not right now." He held her at arm's length. "You sure look pretty, Dawn."

In spite of herself, she blushed. It was as if no time had passed since they'd last seen one another. At that moment, her parents, who'd stayed out of the way and in the kitchen, came into the room. Dawn made a round of introductions.

"We've heard a lot about you," her father said, making Dawn feel self-conscious. She didn't want Brent thinking that all she'd done was babble about him.

"We're glad to have you stay for a few days," her mother added. "Your sister meant a great deal to Dawn, and we will always cherish her memory."

"Thank you," Brent murmured.

Dawn wished that they hadn't mentioned Sandy, especially when she saw a look of sadness cross Brent's face. "Let me show you where you'll be staying," she said hastily.

"Can I help you bring your things in?" her dad asked.

"I'll get them. There's not much—a duffle bag and a big wrapped box." Brent winked at Dawn. "The box is for under your tree."

Eventually, she was able to lead the way down to the basement to the rec room. Just off the rec room her dad had transformed an area into a guest bedroom and bath. She pointed to a plate of cookies on a small table next to the bed. "I baked these myself, in case you get hungry in the middle of the night."

He sampled one of them. "They're delicious."

"How's college?" she asked.

"If it weren't for having to go to classes and studying, I'd like it just fine."

She laughed. "Isn't that what college is all about?" She remembered what he'd told her last summer. "Are you still planning on being a doctor?"

Brent gave a little shrug. "Pre-med looks like it's going to be a lot tougher than I thought. I'm not sure I'm cut out for it."

For some reason, Dawn felt disappointed. She had wanted him to be a doctor and to treat kids with cancer. "What else, then?"

"It's too soon to tell. There are so many courses freshmen have to take that it's hard to think about a major this early on." He gazed down at her. "How's high school?"

"Not all it's cracked up to be. Hardy's so big, a person gets lost."

"No excitement at all?"

She puckered her brow. "One thing." She told him about the new cancer wing dedication and her role in it.

"I'm impressed."

"Don't be. I'll probably embarrass myself by going blank when I have to stand up there and give my speech. Not to mention coming up with something important for the time capsule."

He took a bite out of another cookie. "So what's the game plan for my three-day visit? You going to show me around Columbus?"

"I've got lots of places to take you. Don't worry, you won't get bored."

"I never figured I would be." His blue eyes glowed, and he reached out and ran his thumb along her cheek. A shiver of delight shot up her spine. "Not for a single minute."

* * * * *

The next day Brent drove around Columbus, with Dawn pointing out special sights. In the late afternoon, they stopped by the largest mall, crammed with Christmas shoppers hurrying from store to store. A gigantic tree stood near the entrance of the food court. They stood and watched a tiny train run its course around the tree.

They skirted a long line of small kids

waiting to sit on Santa's lap and miraculously found an empty table. "You hold our place and I'll get us some drinks," Brent told Dawn.

She was watching clusters of people scurry past when, to her surprise, Rhonda called to her. "Help!" Rhonda flopped dramatically onto a chair. "My mother's holding me prisoner and won't let me go until we've bought something for every relative on her list." She straightened. "What are you doing here? I thought you'd be off alone with Brent." She looked around. "Where is he, anyway? I want to see this hunk with my own eyes."

Dawn thought Rhonda was acting overly dramatic. "He went to get us something to drink."

"Is it great having a guy drive all the way from college to visit you? What's it like having him *sleeping* under your roof?"

"Slow down." Dawn glanced up. "Why don't you ask him for yourself? He's right behind you."

"Ask me what?" Brent wanted to know.

Rhonda fairly shot out of the chair, almost knocking Brent backward. "Oh—sorry! I . . . I didn't see you. Hi. I'm Dawn's best friend."

87

Rhonda appeared so flustered, it was hard for Dawn to keep from laughing. "This is Rhonda. I've mentioned her to you in my letters."

Brent grinned. "You take my drink and I'll get another."

"No, no," Rhonda said. "I—um—was just leaving." Behind Brent's back, she made a face like a panting puppy, again causing Dawn to almost burst out laughing. All at once, Rhonda jumped up and down and started waving. "Yoo-hoo! Sharon," she yelled across the crowded food court. "Why look, Dawn, it's Sharon Lewis."

Dawn turned in time to see Sharon and a group of her friends. Sharon glanced coldly from Rhonda, then to Dawn, then to Brent. Her mouth almost dropped open. Dawn groaned and buried her face in her hands. Rhonda was obviously trying to get Sharon to notice Dawn and Brent together.

Sharon tossed her head and marched off into the crowd. "Gee, maybe she didn't see us," Rhonda said with a silly grin. "Oops— my mom's signaling to me. Got to run." She waved good-bye and made her way toward the Christmas tree.

"What was that all about?" Brent looked puzzled.

Bemused, Dawn shook her head. "Believe me, Rhonda defies explanation."

He took a long swig from his cup. "So, she's your best friend?"

"I've known her since the fifth grade and she's pretty much always been there for me." She stopped herself short, realizing who she was talking to and why he might be asking. *Sandy had been her best friend.* She didn't want Brent to think her disloyal. "Not like Sandy, though. Look, all this noise is giving me a headache. Why don't we head for home?" Dawn grabbed her cup and purse and stood up.

Slowly, Brent rose beside her. "Sure," he said. "This place is bugging me too."

He was quiet all during supper. She wasn't sure how to break through his silence. She wasn't even sure if anything was wrong. But she felt anxious, as if they were somehow out of sync.

Dawn slept fitfully and woke very early. She saw a stream of light beneath her door and heard someone moving downstairs. Slipping on her velour robe, she padded down the staircase. In the living room, the Christmas tree lights had been turned on and Brent was sitting on the sofa, staring moodily at the tall evergreen. "Is something wrong?" she asked, coming into the room.

"I didn't mean to wake anyone," he said guiltily.

She sat beside him on the couch. "What's wrong, Brent? Please tell me."

He turned his face and she saw his sadness instantly. He said, "I can't stop thinking about my sister."

Twelve

DAWN longed to make Brent's hurt go away. "I'm sorry if what Rhonda said at the mall about being my best friend upset you."

He shook his head. "That's not it. I mean, I know how you felt about Sandy, and I'd never expect you to not have other friends. And I don't want you to think that I think about my dead sister all the time, because I don't." He shrugged his shoulders and gazed back at the tree. "Maybe it's just 'cause it's Christmas."

"How do you mean?"

He didn't explain right away, but when he did, his voice sounded thick and soft. "Our family's always been big on Christmas. When we were younger, we never had a lot in the way of presents 'cause we never had a lot of money. But we kids never noticed. Mama and Daddy put on a fine celebration. All the kids would sneak into my room on Christmas Eve and we'd talk half the night about what Santa might be bringing us.

"I had a flashlight, and we'd make a tent under the covers and talk about how rich we'd be when we grew up, and how we'd take turns coming to visit each other different Christmases in our mansions." Dawn saw a soft smile cross Brent's face. "Sandy always said she'd have a big white house with a red roof and a big green lawn with a lake in the back. She said she'd have enough bedrooms so that we'd never have to share like we did in our house. And that she'd even build a little house out back for Mama and Daddy to live in when they got really old."

In her mind's eye, Dawn could see Sandy's dream perfectly. It caused a lump to form in her throat, knowing that her friend's dreams could never come true. "She used to talk to me about getting married," Dawn offered. "She said she wanted a big family."

Brent nodded, making the reflection from the tree lights bounce off his blond hair. "That first Christmas . . . after Sandy was gone . . . well, that was the hardest one. We went through the motions. We tried to do all the things we usually did for the holidays, but without her, it just wasn't the same."

Dawn's heart was breaking for him. She knew exactly how he felt. She had cried off and on for months after Sandy died. It hadn't mattered where she was or what she was doing. If something brought the memory of her friend back to her, her eyes would fill with tears. "I wish she were here," she said softly.

Brent stared at the tree and continued. "That first Christmas, late in the afternoon, Daddy and I went out to the cemetery where she's buried. It was really cold. The sky was all gray and the wind kept whipping through the tree branches. There were some snow flurries. Daddy and I just stood there looking down at her headstone. I kept thinking that it wasn't right for the dates of her birth and her death to be so close together. Thirteen years. That's all she had." Brent linked his fingers together and hunched forward on the sofa. "It was the only time I ever saw my dad cry."

The lump in Dawn's throat had grown impossibly large and her eyes swam with tears. "I wish I knew what to say . . ."

He smiled at her wistfully. "There's nothing anyone can say. I had a sister and she died too young." His expression changed. "I really don't sit around thinking about it all the time. I don't want you to think I'm morbid or anything. It's just that it's Christmas, and this is the hardest time of the year for me. I wish I could talk to her one more time, you know?"

Dawn sniffed. "I know what you mean about wanting to talk to her. I'd give just about anything to hear her voice." Brent nodded. All at once, Dawn was struck with an idea. "Wait right here," she told him, scooting off the couch. "I'll be right back."

She hurried up the stairs to her room and rifled through her closet shelf until she found what she was looking for. Quickly, she descended to the living room and returned to the sofa, thrusting a shoebox into Brent's hands. "I want you to have this."

His brow puckered. "You said my Christmas gift was under the tree."

"It's not your Christmas present." She took a deep breath. "It's—it's some of Sandy's things. The stuff she left to me."

He shook his head vigorously and thrust the box onto her lap. "I couldn't. She wanted you to have this stuff."

"I know she gave it to me," Dawn said. "But I think you should take it now. It's a way for you to hold on to her."

Slowly, he took the old shoebox and lifted the lid. The reflection of the tree lights twinkled on the glitter from the popcorn necklace Sandy had made during her stay in the hospital. "Looks pretty bedraggled," Brent said with a half-smile as he held it up.

"It's a work of art," Dawn countered, returning his smile.

His hands played over the combs and hair ribbons. "She sure liked fixing her hair. I remember how she cried when all of it fell out from the chemo." He held up a handful of the colorful ribbons, gently brought them to his nose, and sniffed. "They still smell like her hair," he said in wonderment.

Dawn wasn't so sure. After all, they'd been shut inside the box for years and stored in her attic until this past summer. But if the items smelled that way to him, she didn't want to take away from the comfort they might provide.

"You sure you want me to take these?" he asked. "She gave them to you."

She felt her heart clutch, and for a moment she almost backed down. But seeing his fascination with the items and understanding how much they meant to him gave her courage. "I'll just hold on to a few things for memory's sake. I want you to take the rest. You're her brother and some-day you can show them to your kids and tell them all about their special aunt."

Dawn saw that his eyes looked misty. She glanced quickly down into the box and rummaged through it. Finally, she settled on one set of combs, the popcorn necklace, and the page from the Bible imprinted with Ecclesiastes 3.

He closed the lid and laid the shoebox next to him on the sofa. He raised his hand and stroked Dawn's hair, all the while gazing into her eyes. "Thank you, Dawn."

"We both loved her," Dawn said. "It's only right we should share her."

He pulled her into his arms and they clung to each other with a soft and quiet tenderness. Dawn had the feeling that Sandy was somehow in the room with them, holding them in arms big enough for both.

*   *   *   *   *

She'd opened the gift from Brent the night before he left, and she was crazy about the book bag and sweatshirt bearing the emblem from his college, West Virginia Tech. Once he had left for home, she moped around, but by Christmas morning, she woke up excited about the holiday ahead of her.

All the time they were opening gifts that morning, Rob seemed distracted. He left early to pick up Katie and bring her back for Christmas dinner. "We're going to open our presents to each other together," he explained, grabbing his keys and darting out the door.

When Katie and Rob came back, they came in through the kitchen, where Dawn was helping her mom and dad prepare Christmas dinner. "Just in time to peel potatoes," Mrs. Rochelle announced.

Dawn took one look at Katie and knew something was going on. Katie's face looked radiant. Dawn looked to her brother, who appeared equally happy. "Okay, you guys, what's up? You both look like you're ready to bust." Her parents stopped their work and came over to investigate.

Katie glanced at Rob and he nodded. She held out her hand. "Rob asked me to marry him, and I said yes," Katie announced. From her finger, a diamond glittered.

Thirteen

"**E**NGAGED! Yikes! You mean your brother went and got engaged? Does that mean he's definitely not going to wait for me?" Rhonda asked. Rhonda and Dawn were sitting in Dawn's bedroom the day after Christmas, checking over her gifts, when Dawn broke the big news.

"I know it's hard to accept, Rhonda, but you'll just have to. You're a big girl now." Dawn kept a straight face as she spoke. Rhonda's hopeless crush on Dawn's older brother had long been a standing joke between them.

"I'm wounded." Rhonda flopped dramatically on the bed. "But if it can't be me, then I'm glad it's Katie."

"Me too." Dawn shifted to the bed and sat cross-legged. The news had really lifted her spirits, especially since she'd been missing

Sandy so much. The terrible sadness of the one was offset by the joy of the other. Marriage meant a new beginning, and Dawn was thrilled about the engagement.

"The wedding was all we talked about yesterday. Me and Mom and Katie spent the afternoon making plans and lists. It's going to be so much fun, because this time things are just right."

"In other words, you mean Darcy, the snob, isn't his fianceé."

"That's not nice," Dawn scolded.

"You never liked Darcy and you know it."

"She just wasn't the one for Rob." Dawn also knew that Darcy had never cared much for her. Nothing had ever been said outright, but deep down, Dawn had always suspected that Rob had broken his engagement to Darcy because she couldn't accept Dawn's illness.

"So when's the wedding?" Rhonda wanted to know.

"At the end of June. And they're holding the reception in the Conservatory gardens."

"Oh, that's *soooo* romantic."

"Everything's romantic to you."

"I guess you'll be in the wedding."

"Katie's asked me to be the Maid of Honor." Dawn beamed a smile.

"June's six months away. It seems like *forever*," Rhonda lamented.

"Katie and Mom say there are a million things to do. Katie has to shop for a gown and the bridesmaids' dresses. She and Rob have to make out a guest list, reserve the church, hire a caterer, decide where to go on their honeymoon, and find an apartment."

"A honeymoon. How romantic." Rhonda was beginning to sound like a broken record. "I *will* be invited, won't I?" She sat up and leaned into Dawn's face.

"I doubt they'll want you on their honeymoon."

"Very funny." Rhonda scooted backward. "I mean, I want to come to the wedding."

"How could we leave you off the list? Impossible."

"Good. I have to plan what to wear. Who knows if a cute guy will show up or not?"

Rhonda would never change. "Good thing we've given you plenty of time."

"Have you heard anything from Brent?"

"He called to wish me a merry Christmas." She'd already told Rhonda about Brent's visit, leaving out the part about their discussion of Sandy. Their conversations about Sandy had been too personal, too private. Why was it so easy for her to discuss Sandy with Brent and yet she felt unable to even mention her name to Jake? She knew it went deeper than the fact that Brent was Sandy's brother. It was as if she were protecting Jake from the realities of her cancer. As if the truth would somehow drive him away.

"I'm actually looking forward to school starting." Rhonda changed the subject. "We get to practice driving during Driver's Ed. In another two months, I'll get my license."

"Lucky you." Dawn was excited about school starting again too, but not because of Driver's Ed. Dawn couldn't wait to see Jake again. She wondered if he thought about her half as much as she thought of him.

* * * * * *

School had been in session for a week before Dawn saw Jake long enough to talk to him. She was on her way to Driver's Ed and he was on his way to the gym. "How was your holiday?" she asked.

"All right. And yours?"

"Fine." The day was blustery and cold, even though the sun was shining. She hugged her coat closer. "My brother got engaged," she added, then immediately felt dumb. What could Jake possibly care? He didn't even know Rob.

"But *you're* still unattached, aren't you?"

She glanced at him quickly and saw that he was teasing her.

"Of course I am." She felt her cheeks flush and hoped he'd think the redness was due to the wind. "Doesn't soccer season start soon?"

"The first of March. But the team's practicing every day after school. I heard they're holding cheerleading try-outs in March. And I remember that you were a great cheerleader. Are you going to try out?"

Dawn hadn't even considered it. She figured that since Sharon was the captain, she'd never have a chance. Plus, she still had clinic visits to work into her schedule. "Not this year. I'm not sure I'm one of the squad's favorite people."

Jake stopped and looked at her with surprise. "You're wrong. A lot of kids in this school admire you. Since that article came out in the paper, plenty of them have asked about you."

Terrific, she thought darkly. She was a celebrity because she had cancer. "I can

102

think of other ways I'd rather be remembered."

"People are curious. They want to know more about you."

Dawn groaned. It was the *last* thing she wanted. "Well, do me a favor and tell them it's not worth knowing about. It was horrible and now it's over—end of story." Nervously, she peeked at her watch. "I've got to run or I'll be late to class."

As she hurried off, she realized that she'd probably made a bad impression on Jake. *What does it matter?* she thought. After all, he had only been making polite conversation on his way to the gym. He'd always think of her as "that girl who had cancer."

* * * * * *

"Don't you just *love* it?" Katie asked as she led Dawn from room to room in the empty apartment.

February sunlight poured through double banks of windows in the living room of the old Victorian house that had been converted to apartments. The oak floors needed polishing and the walls needed painting, but Dawn could see the potential in the spacious rooms with high ceilings and carved doors. "I think it's super. When will you move in?"

"Rob and I figure that I can move in next month and together we can fix it up, buy some furniture, then he can move in with me after the wedding."

Dawn poked her head into one of the rooms. An old-fashioned bathtub with claw feet stood in the middle of the floor, and a pedestal sink stood beside it. "There's no shower."

Katie laughed. "We're lucky to have working plumbing. This place is over a hundred years old. But we both think it's so neat."

Since graduating, Rob had been working for a local engineering firm, and Katie still had her job at the hospital. It seemed that all they ever talked about was their future. Dawn walked through the bathroom into a smaller area that led to the room Katie had said was the master bedroom. "What's this space for? It's too big for a closet."

"That's the nursery. In Victorian times, it often adjoined the main bedroom so the baby could be tended to in the middle of the night."

"Cool. Does this mean you and Rob are

going to have a baby right away?"

Katie laughed. "No way! We plan to wait awhile."

"Don't wait too long. Who knows, maybe I'll get married and have a baby right away. Then mine and yours will be close to the same age. Think about it—I'd be an aunt and a mother all at once." Dawn was joking, but even as she was speaking, she saw Katie's expression change from one of smiling to one of concern. "What did I say?" Dawn asked. "What's wrong? Are you thinking I'll never find a guy who'll want to marry me?"

"It's nothing like that," Katie said. She took Dawn's hand sympathetically. "I thought you knew."

"Knew what?"

"Honey, with all the chemo and radiation you've had, it's highly unlikely you'll ever be able to have children of your own."

Fourteen

"IS what Katie told me the truth, Dr. Sinclair? Will I never be able to have a baby?" Dawn sat in her doctor's office, her hands gripping the arms of her chair. She'd finished her latest round of bloodwork that afternoon in the outpatient clinic. Then she'd gone directly to his office to ask him the question that burned in her mind.

The doctor studied her with a kind face. His hair was gray at the temples, and the lines around his eyes looked deeper than when she'd first become his patient, almost four years before. "Some of your earlier chemo and radiation protocols will have an effect on the reproduction process," he said.

She felt a sinking sensation in the pit of her stomach. "Then it's true."

"More than likely. It's possible that you will be able to have children, but it still might not be advisable."

Tears sprang instantly to Dawn's eyes. She glanced quickly away. She'd never thought much about having children. She'd simply figured it was something she'd do eventually—if she got married. If she lived. "Why didn't anyone tell me?"

"Frankly, it never came up. We were never attempting to hide it from you, but you were so sick that it hardly seemed important." He sighed and leaned back in his swivel chair.

"Later on, when it becomes necessary, there will be tests you can take to determine your fertility."

"But to never have a family!" she blurted.

"Dawn, hundreds of couples never have children and still have a very satisfying married life. And there are other options— like adoption, for instance."

She almost put her hands over her ears. She didn't want to hear about "options." In fact, she didn't even want to discuss it any further. Here she was, not quite sixteen, and already she was being forced to look into a future that was upside-down and backward. Dawn stood up. "It's later than I thought. My mom will be looking for me."

"Don't run off. I think you should talk

107

about this. We have trained professionals on staff who can help you come to terms with it."

She knew what he was suggesting. She should see one of the hospital's counselors. Well, she didn't want to. She didn't want to face prodding and questioning about her innermost feelings with a stranger. "I've got to go." She left his office as fast as she could.

In the car, Dawn stared gloomily out the window. Her mother interrupted her dark mood. "Rhonda called to say that she passed her driver's test and wanted to go out for pizza tonight. I told her you were getting bloodwork done and that you'd call her when you got home. Would you like to go off with her tonight? She sure sounded eager."

Dawn had forgotten that this was the day Rhonda was going for her driver's license. How could she have? Rhonda had talked about nothing else for days. "I'll call her, but yes, I'd like to go."

"Honey, what's wrong?" Her mother's voice sounded concerned. "Did everything go all right at the hospital?"

"Everything went fine."

"But I can tell something's bothering you." In spite of telling herself not to cry,

Dawn felt a tear trickle down her cheek. Alarmed, her mother pulled over into a grocery store parking lot and turned off the engine. "What's wrong? Tell me."

Haltingly, Dawn revealed what she'd learned. She'd been carrying it around inside of her for weeks, and the discussion with Dr. Sinclair hadn't helped at all. "I feel like I've been robbed," she told her mother. "As if someone stole something from me and I can't get it back."

Her mother said nothing.

"You knew, didn't you?" Dawn asked. "You and Daddy knew all along. Why did you keep it a secret? Why didn't you say something to me?" She couldn't hide the sense of betrayal in her voice.

"You were thirteen, Dawn, and fighting for your life. It hardly seemed relevant. All that mattered was that you lived. If you'd had a kind of cancer that meant you'd lose an arm or a leg in order to save your life, we'd certainly have agreed. We knew that the medications they were giving you were potent enough to damage or possibly destroy your reproductive system, but at the time, it didn't matter."

"Maybe it would have mattered to me!"

"Think back. You were a scared little girl,

109

still collecting teddy bears. How could you have made such a choice at that time?"

Rationally, she knew her mother was right. They'd made the only choices they could. She wasn't angry with her parents. Or her doctors. She was simply *angry* over what she hadn't had any choice about. It was the same kind of anger she'd felt when Sandy had died. And Marlee. Helpless, frustrated anger—anger at life because it just wasn't fair.

Her mother took a deep breath and touched Dawn's shoulder. "I'm so sorry, honey. I'd give anything if it had been me instead of you."

"You would have traded places with me?"

"In a heartbeat. You're my daughter and I love you very much."

Dawn felt a softening inside her. She saw that her mother was hurting, and for the first time, she realized how much her illness had affected her whole family. Yet they had survived it. All of them. And for the most part, they were happy. Her parents were together, Rob was getting married, and she was alive. "If some guy ever wants to marry me, what do I tell him?"

"The truth. If he loves you, it won't matter." Dawn couldn't imagine it not mattering. "Listen," her mother added, "when I was pregnant with Rob, all my doctor could tell me was that the baby was big and had a strong heartbeat. Now, they can tell if it's a boy or a girl, if there are genetic defects—why, doctors can even operate on a fetus while it's still in its mother's womb.

"Think about it, Dawn. Who knows what kind of technology they'll have available by the time you're completely grown and ready to get married and have a baby! Don't consider childbirth for you a closed book. You've got to think positively. You've got to think about what you do have, instead of what you don't."

Hesitantly, Dawn nodded. She knew her mother was right.

"All right," she said softly. "I won't think about it any more."

"You have a wonderful future ahead of you. You're alive. That's worth everything."

Her mother started the car, and together they drove the rest of the way home in thoughtful silence.

*　*　*　*　*

Hardy High's soccer season started on a

chilly, sunny Friday afternoon in March. Jake Macka scored a hat trick and three goals, and Hardy won four to one. Dawn cheered from the stands and when the game was over, Jake called her over to the side of the field.

"I'll wait for you," Rhonda said, juggling her car keys.

Rhonda's mother had allowed her to use her car that day so that she and Dawn could stay for the game.

Jake was all smiles as Dawn approached. "You played a great game," she told him.

"Help me celebrate."

"Me?"

He made a production of looking around. "I don't see anybody else. You were cheering for me, weren't you?"

Her heart began to hammer. "How can I help you celebrate?"

"Go to a movie with me tomorrow night."

Words seemed trapped in her throat. "All right," she managed.

He grinned. "I'll call you tomorrow."

She watched him jog off to rejoin his team on the way to the locker room. *Jake had asked her out!*

"What's up?" Rhonda asked, coming up beside her.

"Jake asked me for a date."

Rhonda's eyes grew large. "Wow! Lucky you."

Dawn couldn't stop smiling. "Yeah. Lucky me." And in her heart, she meant it.

Fifteen

DAWN scarcely saw the movie on Saturday night. She only remembered the complete sense of contentment she felt sitting in the dark theater, sharing a jumbo bag of buttered popcorn with Jake. Sometimes their hands brushed as they went for the bag together, and once, during an especially tense part of the movie, he put his arm around her. When the film was over, he took her hand and led her up the aisle and out into the damp, chilly March night. "How about a soda?" he asked. "All that popcorn made me thirsty."

Since she didn't want the evening to end, she agreed quickly. He drove her to one of the popular hangouts, and she didn't mind one bit when heads turned as they entered. From the corner of her eye she saw Sharon, but she was with another guy, so Dawn figured that whatever had been going on between her and Jake was long since over.

Jake showed Dawn to a booth toward the back and slid in beside her. After the waitress took their order, he smiled and asked, "What did you think of the movie?"

"It was good." She hoped he didn't ask any details, since she couldn't remember any. "How's soccer going?"

"Great. We play twice next week. Will you be there?"

"I wouldn't miss it." An awkward silence fell and she racked her brain for something witty to say. Why did her brain turn to mush every time she was with Jake? He probably thought she was a real dope.

"I guess that big ceremony's coming up soon." He broke the strained silence. "The one I read about."

"Next month—the weekend after Easter. I'm glad Easter comes late this year. It gives me more time."

"Do you know what you're going to put in the time capsule yet?"

For a moment, Dawn wasn't sure she wanted to be discussing this with him. After all, it did have to do with her cancer. But she quickly decided to pretend that the capsule wasn't connected with cancer at all.

She would pretend that it was more just a place for preserving fragments of the past for posterity. "I've been thinking hard about it. It's a big responsibility. What do you think people would want to know about us a hundred years from now?"

"How about a story on Hardy's great soccer team?" He grinned impishly.

"People may not even play sports in a hundred years. We may all be video game freaks and never leave the front of our television sets. We'll all have fat rear ends from sitting all the time and fat thumbs from pressing game buttons."

He grimaced at her suggestion. "Let's hope not."

"Do you have any suggestions? I'm willing to hear them."

"How about some music?"

"Explain."

"You could make a cassette of today's top hits. That way kids in the twenty-first century can hear what kids from today thought was cool."

She liked his idea. "They'll probably think our stuff is weird. I know when I hear the music my parents liked, I can't believe it."

"You should try listening to what your grandparents liked. Talk about weird!"

They laughed together. "I could use some help making the cassette," she said. "Would you help me?"

"Sure." His brown eyes reminded her of melted pools of dark, rich chocolate. "Do you have a tape deck that can make dubs? Maybe I could come over and bring some blank tapes. How about next Saturday?"

"That's fine with me." If he'd suggested they start at two in the morning, it would have been fine with her.

He drove her home, and at the door, she secretly hoped he would kiss her. He looked as if he might, and her heart thudded in anticipation. But at the last moment, he backed off, said goodnight, and left.

She went to her room and relived every moment of her date with him as she undressed for bed. Impulsively, she opened her desk drawer and fumbled for her diary. She had two. The first was full of her thoughts and impressions from when she was first diagnosed with cancer. Absently, she thumbed through it, rereading the details of her ordeal, her times at camp, her memories of Sandy, her relapse and readmission to the hospital for her bone marrow transplant.

She saw the parts Rob had entered on

her behalf, when she'd been too sick to write anything. She reread the entries about Marlee and Brent, and Marlee's funeral. It didn't seem right to put something about Jake and her new life in it. She tossed aside the older diary and opened the newer one.

March 18

It's strange to write about Jake. Who would have thought that he would ever come back into my life? Even though so much has happened to me in the past years, even though I've met so many new guys—Mike, Greg, Brent—Jake is still the one. I don't know why, but ever since fifth grade, I've liked him. It's the brown eyes, I think. None of the others had brown eyes. Whenever Jake looks at me, I feel like melting. Go figure!

I wonder where Brent fits in all of this? I still care about him. Every time he calls, it's like we've never been apart. We pick up right where we left off the last time. How can that be? How can I like Brent so much and still feel the way I do about Jake?

I guess Katie's right. Sixteen (almost!) is too young to decide anything about a boy. Now if only I can get the message through to my heart . . .

* * * * *

Dawn woke up Monday morning with a scratchy, raw throat. Her mother insisted she forget about school and spend the day in bed. She didn't want to. She wanted to go to school to see Jake, but there was no changing her mother's mind.

By that night, Dawn was running a fever and felt weak and achy all over. She was too sick to even talk to Rhonda when she called. All through the night, Dawn tossed and turned, and by the next morning she had a hacking cough and a tightness in her chest that made it difficult to breathe.

She staggered to the bathroom, convinced that a warm shower would make her feel better. But when she shed her nightgown and looked into the mirror, her heart wedged in her throat. A fine red rash covered her arms and torso. She started shaking so violently that she had to grab ahold of the sink for support.

Dawn knew what the rash meant. She'd

119

read too many pamphlets and booklets following her transplant. A rash was often the very first sign of bone marrow rejection.

Sixteen

"**D**ON'T panic," Dr. Sinclair told Dawn as he listened to her chest through his stethoscope in the Emergency Room.

"I *am* panicking." Dawn's voice sounded raspy. She wadded the sheet covering her with her fists. On the other side of the door, her parents and Rob waited for Dr. Sinclair to finish his checkup. She'd seen how scared they looked when she showed them the rash along her arms. They'd left for the hospital immediately, and Dr. Sinclair had met them in the emergency room. "Am I rejecting? Please tell me the truth, Dr. Sinclair."

"I don't like what I'm hearing. I want some X-rays, but I'm sure you've got pneumonia."

He had avoided answering her question. "Am I rejecting?"

"It's too soon to tell." He straightened. "I'm checking you in."

Tears swam in her eyes. "I don't want to be back in the hospital. Everything's been going so well until now."

"No choice, Dawn. As you know, the immune-suppressants make you more vulnerable to infections. You need to be here for your own safety. I'm going to increase your suppressant medications and start antibiotics and oxygen. I want you here where I can keep a close eye on you." He gently squeezed her shoulder. "You'll have to go into isolation, too. I'm sorry. There's no other alternative. I'll go tell your family and start the paperwork to move you upstairs."

She tried to hold back her tears. Breathing was already difficult enough without crying. *Why? Why is this happening to me?* For a while, things had been going so smoothly that she'd almost forgotten about her health. She was doing well in school, she'd had a date with Jake—she suddenly remembered another reason to feel bad—her birthday was coming up. She'd made plans to go take the test for her learner's permit. Now, she'd be spending her birthday in the hospital. And if she *had*

rejected the bone marrow, there was no
hope left for her at all.

*   *   *   *   *

The oxygen tent, with its fine mist of
oxygen mixed with decongestants, did help
Dawn's breathing. From inside the plastic
enclosure, everything outside looked fuzzy
to her, as if people were moving around in
a fog. IV lines, inserted in the back of her
hand, regulated a controlled flow of potent
medications into her bloodstream. The pain
medication she was taking made her feel
spacey, but it did help her deal with the
pain left over from her most recent ordeal—
a spinal tap, which would tell the doctors
whether there was cancer in her system.

The only visitors allowed were her imme-
diate family, and they had to wear masks
and green paper gowns and head coverings.
Germs—any kind of germs—were her ene-
mies. Because Katie was a nurse, and
because Rob had called her from the emergency room, she and Rob came in together.
Dawn reached out for Rob. He took her hand
and held it tightly. "You're going to lick this
thing," he said. His voice was upbeat, but
she saw genuine fear in his eyes.

123

"Dr. Sinclair said my bone marrow needs a little extra help. He said that the pneumonia is taxing it to the max, but I know it's going to hang in there for me." She wanted to assure him that he wasn't responsible for what was happening to her. The bone marrow—*his* marrow—wasn't at fault for her troubles.

"It had better hang in there. But if you need more, just say the word."

"Katie, I'm sorry we can't go shopping for bridesmaid dresses this weekend, the way we planned."

"That's not important. All that matters is you getting well." Katie's blue eyes looked serious above her mask. "I've asked my supervisor to assign me to your case, and I'm going to move some things into the nurses' quarters so I can be close-by."

Knowing that Katie was going to take care of her made Dawn feel secure. "Just like you did before," she said. "Will you call Rhonda for me? Will you tell her I'll call just as soon as I can?"

"Of course I will. Is there anyone else?"

She thought of Jake and Brent. As much as she hated Jake knowing, she realized Rhonda would tell him. As for Brent, she didn't want him called yet. There was nothing he could do but worry. "I'll tell my other friends," she told Rob and Katie. "I don't want them to freak out over this. I'm sure it's only a temporary setback."

"Whatever you want," Katie said. What Dawn wanted was to be well, to be back home, to have this nightmare behind her.

"You get some rest," Rob added. "Just concentrate all your strength on recovering. You've come too far to be sidelined now."

Over the next week, Dawn practiced the imaging techniques she'd been taught. She imagined the pneumonia virus being tracked down by her white blood cells—her non-leukemic white blood cells—and zapped into oblivion. Focusing on the destruction of the virus *did* make her feel better emotionally.

Cards began to arrive for her. Several from Rhonda and girls in her classes, and one from Jake. He'd even scribbled a note inside. It said: *"We won both matches, but I only scored one goal. See what happens when you're not in the stands for me to impress? Get well, Jake."* She traced his signature with her fingertips and wished with all her heart that things could be different, that she could be normal and healthy.

At the end of the week, Dr. Sinclair took down the oxygen tent but insisted she remain in isolation. Her condition was still too vulnerable to ordinary germs, and her bone marrow needed all the help it could get. Katie saw to it that she got a phone in her room. It had to be specially sterilized, but Dawn loved being able to connect with the outside world again. She called Rhonda. "When can I come see you?" her friend asked.

"Dr. Sinclair says that I can have outside visitors anytime, but they'll have to garb up."

"You mean dress in those funny little paper outfits?"

"Yes. I know they're hardly a fashion statement."

"I'm glad you still have your sense of humor." Rhonda went on to fill Dawn in on all the latest from school, but all the news only depressed her. She felt like a runner who'd been yanked out of a race and now had to play catch-up. Life was passing her by, and there was nothing she could do about it. A wave of pity swept through her, and after Rhonda hung up, she had a long cry. She was tired, so very tired, of standing on the outside, looking in.

When the phone rang later that night, she was still feeling low. She didn't feel like talking to anyone, but she answered it because she couldn't think of any other way to make it stop ringing. Her caller was Brent.

"I called your house to say hi, and your mom told me how to reach you. Why didn't you let me know what was going on?"

His voice sounded hurt and she was sorry. "I wanted to tell you myself. Once I was better."

"Are you better?"

"I think so. But I sure don't look so hot." Her face and lower limbs were retaining fluid, so she looked plump and puffy.

"You getting out soon?"

"Dr. Sinclair won't say. I hope so. I'm so far behind in school and all."

"You sound really down."

"I am." There was no use hiding the truth from Brent. If anyone understood, he did. "I'm just sick of the whole mess."

"Now, you're not giving up, are you?"

"No," she said, but without much conviction.

" 'Cause one of the reasons I called was to tell you that the committee in charge of that dedication ceremony has invited my whole family to come."

Dawn's grip tightened on the receiver. Up until that moment, she'd forgotten all about the upcoming ceremony.

"You're all coming?"

"I didn't think Daddy would want to at first. He's always held a grudge against the doctors and the hospital for not making Sandy well. But he surprised me and said he wanted all of us to go." She heard him pause. "So, I reckon the bottom line is that you have to get well and get out of the hospital, Dawn. We're all coming to that ceremony, and we want to hear your speech."

Seventeen

THE next afternoon Dawn looked up and saw Jake standing at her doorway. For a moment, her breath caught and she could scarcely breathe. He looked handsome, even with a green mask on.

He looked healthy—and so out of place.

"Hi," he said. "Up for a visitor?"

No! her mind screamed. "I—I—sure. Come in," she replied hesitantly.

He entered the room cautiously, eyeing the equipment and hospital paraphernalia. "I—um—I've never been in a hospital before," he confessed.

"I don't recommend it," she said. In her mind she was thinking, *Welcome to my world, Jake.* She felt awkward and self-conscious and wished she were wearing one of her cute nightshirts instead of the hospital gown that tied behind her neck.

"Sorry, I have to wear this thing." She apologized for the mask that covered her mouth.

"Rhonda said you had pneumonia."

Dawn was a tiny bit relieved. At least pneumonia was something that could happen to anybody. Maybe she wouldn't have to make a big deal about her cancer. "It's clearing up," she said.

"I brought you something." He pulled a small shopping bag from behind his back and grinned sheepishly. The tips of his ears were bright red, and Dawn could tell he was self-conscious, unsure of himself.

"You brought me a present?"

"Only one's a present. The other is something we talked about doing together."

Mystified, she opened the bag and took out a small, cuddly white teddy bear. She rubbed her cheek against the soft fur.

"He's adorable. Thanks."

"I remembered that you liked teddy bears."

"I had a whole collection once. And I still have Mr. Ruggers."

"Mr. Ruggers?"

"He's my favorite. Left over from my crib days."

Jake laughed. "I had a stuffed football and a blanket that I dragged around."

Imagining Jake as a toddler made her go all soft inside. She thought back to when they'd been in fifth grade and how crazy she'd been about him. And then she'd gotten leukemia. Five years was a long time to have a crush on somebody. "What else did you bring me?" She poked inside the bag.

"It's that cassette of today's top hits for the time capsule. I hope you don't mind that I taped the songs without you. I—um—didn't know if you'd still want to do it. If you don't want to use it, it's okay. I only wanted to help out."

She had completely forgotten their discussion about it! She cleared her throat. "I appreciate it. Really. It's just that I don't know if I'll be attending that ceremony." She fiddled with the cassette, wishing he'd drop the subject.

"Why not?"

"I'm not sure how all this is going to turn out, Jake. I don't know if I'll be released by then or not." Telling him felt awkward and painful. It was an admission that her hospitalization was more complicated than pneumonia.

"Oh." He sounded shocked. "I didn't think . . . I mean, I just figured you'd be fine."

"It's no big deal. Relapses happen."

"But you will be all right again, won't you?"

"Probably so. I'm used to this, you know."

"Are you saying it can happen again after this?"

"Maybe. No one knows." She hated having to tell him the truth. All of a sudden, she wished he'd never come to visit her.

"The truth is I'm getting sick and tired of it all."

"You sound as if you're giving up."

Dawn felt a flare of irritation. "You don't understand what my life is like! You're healthy and you can come and go as you please. There's nothing holding you back. I *hate* going through this over and over. Sick. Well. Relapse. Sick. Well. Sick." She ticked her hospitalizations off on her fingers. "Don't you understand that every time it happens it gets harder and harder to keep on smiling?" Dawn felt tears filling her eyes. Quickly she glanced away.

"How could I know what you've been through? You never talk to me about it. You just tell me everything is 'fine.' You make me feel like I should apologize for being well," Jake said.

"That's dumb!"

"No, it's not." Jake sounded angry. "What's

dumb is you giving up. What's dumb is you acting like this setback is the end of the world. What's dumb is me standing here arguing with someone who won't even *try*."

"Well, at least you're free to *leave*," she snapped.

"Is that what you want?"

"You bet. I didn't ask you to come, and I'm not asking you to stay."

"Then fine. I'm leaving."

She watched him turn on his heel and stalk out of the room. For a moment she sat in stunned silence while waves of pain washed over her. The pain wasn't the same as the pain from chemo and needles and cancer. She was accustomed to that kind of hurt. This was a deeper kind of pain. This was the pain of feeling her heart breaking in half as Jake Macka walked out of her life.

Eighteen

"HI, Little Lady," a man's voice said from Dawn's doorway. "They told me down at the nurses' station that you were a patient. And they told me that today was an especially good day to visit. The word down at the nurses' station is that it's your birthday—your sixteenth, they say."

"Dr. Ben! What are you doing here?" Dawn struggled to sit up in bed. She hadn't seen Dr. Ben, director of the cancer camp, since the previous summer, when she'd been a counselor in training.

"Occasionally, I work here." He came alongside her bed and took her hand. "I just admitted a newly diagnosed patient from my private practice. She's twelve and a cute kid. Reminds me a little of you."

"Poor kid."

He laughed. "Poor *me!* I can't imagine

having another Dawn playing pranks on me."

She couldn't help smiling. "We got you pretty good, didn't we?"

"You and that Chandler girl first. Then you and Mike. And I can't forget Marlee Hodges either."

"I didn't have anything to do with that one."

"She was in your cabin." He dragged a chair over and sat down. "How are you feeling?"

"Better." That was partly true anyway. She was feeling physically better. But inside, she still hurt over Jake. And she couldn't make that hurt go away, no matter how hard she tried.

Dr. Ben studied her thoughtfully, then asked, "You're feeling a little blue, aren't you?"

His perception surprised her. "You're a hard person to fool."

"Want to talk about it?"

His white lab coat and necktie made him look too professional. She was used to seeing him in a T-shirt, shorts, and his favorite baseball cap. Then she noticed that his ballpoint pen had left a glob of ink on the pocket of his lab coat. Somehow, the stain made her feel more comfortable, less formal. "No one understands what my life is like, Dr. Ben. The only people who really understood—Sandy, even Marlee—are dead." Dawn picked at her blanket. "When I got sick this time, when I saw that rash, I freaked. I—I thought I was rejecting, and I knew I couldn't take it anymore. I'm so tired of this hospital. I want to be well. You know—normal, like other sixteen-year-olds."

Dawn sighed. She had tried to forget that this was her birthday. She and Rhonda had made great plans—shopping, a movie, and dinner, and knowing Rhonda, she would probably work in some boy-watching, too. Now the whole thing had been postponed indefinitely. She looked at Dr. Ben's kind face. "I just want to have a normal life," she said wistfully.

"Hmmm. I think I know what you mean," he said. "Do you know why I decided to be a pediatric oncologist, Dawn?"

She shook her head. "I can't understand why anyone would want to be. How can you watch kids die?"

"I had an older brother who died from leukemia. That was back in the 60s, when the diagnosis was usually an automatic death sentence."

"I didn't know . . ." She thought of Rob and wondered how she would have felt if this had happened to him instead of her.

"Peter was athletic and smart. I was puny and bookish. Watching him die, seeing how it affected my parents' lives, really influenced me. I thought that by becoming a doctor, I might be able to help kids like him."

"That's the way Sandy's brother feels," Dawn said softly.

"It's hard to stand by and watch people you love suffer," he continued. "You feel like there's something you should be doing to make a difference. You watch people you love die, and you feel guilty because you're still alive."

Dawn felt her cheeks redden. Hadn't she'd felt *exactly* that way? Hadn't she wondered why she'd been left alive while her friends had died?

"Sometimes it's hard to be left behind," she replied.

"We doctors wish we could cure everyone. Every time we lose a patient, it hurts, because it reminds us that we're only human too. The good news is that because of research, because of all kinds of new drugs, some forms of leukemia have a

137

seventy percent cure rate. In Peter's day, it was less than thirty percent."

"You mean we're human guinea pigs."

"When traditional therapies fail, when there's no other choice, yes. People are given experimental drugs and techniques. Your bone marrow transplant was highly experimental in the 70s. Today, such procedures are far more common. And because of immune suppressant drug research, we have successful transplants between non-blood-relative donors. There's the National Marrow Donor Registry to help make genetic matches between organ donors and recipients. If a person wants to be a marrow donor, all he has to do is take a simple blood test. The results are programmed into the data banks, and doctors can search for possible matches for their most critical patients. Sometimes we get lucky and find a match. Believe me, it's a gift of life to someone who needs it."

His eyes looked owlish behind large-framed glasses. "Did you know that we have a survivor support group here at the hospital?"

"Katie told me about it." Dawn didn't want to admit that she'd resisted attending.

"Believe it or not, now that the cure

rate's gone up in cancer victims, so have problems of adjustment."

"What do you mean?"

He placed his hand on her shoulder. "It's sort of like soldiers attempting to readjust to civilian life after the trauma of war. That adjustment can be tough. Sometimes it helps to talk to others who've had similar experiences, so the adjustment can be made more easily."

"I just don't know where I fit in, Dr. Ben. I'm tired of having cancer. I want it to be over forever."

"You should check out the group. You're good at helping people. I remember the first time I saw you at cancer camp. You were with the little Chandler girl, and the two of you made quite a team. You befriended Greg and Mike—no small feat. Mike was a very angry, bitter kid about having his leg amputated. But somehow you two cut through his armor and drew him out."

"That was mostly Sandy's doing."

"It was the two of you. He came back to camp even after Sandy was gone. And you were the person Marlee wanted with her during her hospitalization. No, Dawn." His eyes sparkled mischievously behind his thick glasses. "Like it or not, you have a gift for working with people. You have the gift of caring. You'd better watch out. You may end up becoming a doctor too."

"What's this? Are we adding a new medical recruit to our staff?"

Dawn and Dr. Ben looked up to see Dr. Sinclair in the doorway. He waved some papers at her. "These are the results of your latest bloodwork. It looks perfect. So you can take the worried look off your face and call your mother to come get you. I'm kicking you out, Dawn Rochelle."

Nineteen

A balmy April breeze ruffled Dawn's hair as she sat on the stage, facing an audience seated in folding chairs on the hospital lawn. At the podium, the mayor was giving his speech, but Dawn scarcely heard him. She would be next, and her mouth felt cotton-dry. Other dignitaries sat on the stage with her. A photographer and a TV cameraman skirted the audience of a hundred, taking pictures and a videotape of the event.

On a table beside the podium Dawn saw the metal box that was to be the time capsule. Her fingers brushed the edge of the bag by her feet, holding the treasures for the capsule. Propped next to the capsule was the gold-plated shovel the mayor would use to scoop out the first spadeful of dirt, marking the groundbreaking for the new cancer wing.

In the distance, she saw green, manicured grounds and patches of daffodils waving in the soft spring breeze. Overhead, the sky sparkled blue, freshly washed by an April shower. Dawn's eyes skimmed the audience. Her parents, Rob, Katie, and Rhonda were sitting in the front row.

Right before spring break, Dawn had decided to fill out a schedule card for the next school year. But when she'd shown it to Rhonda, her friend looked aghast. "Why all the science and math courses? I *hate* science and math. We'll never have any classes together if you stick to this schedule!"

"I need them for college," Dawn explained with determination. "I'm thinking about going into medicine."

"You want to be a *doctor?*"

"Don't look so shocked. I know more than most first-year med students already. Heck, I figure I'm halfway to a degree by now."

"All right—I won't complain," Rhonda told her with a grin. "I'm just glad you're making plans again."

From the front row, Rhonda fluttered her fingertips and made a face at Dawn up on the stage. Dawn quickly glanced away. She didn't want to have a giggle fit, and if anyone could start one in her, it was Rhonda.

Her gaze fell on Jake, who sat in the very end seat in the last row. Dawn had almost fallen over when he'd asked if he could come for the ceremony, especially after the harsh words they'd had at the hospital.

"I'm sure it'll be fine," she'd told him stiffly over the phone.

"Good," he'd replied. "I'll see you there."

On the other side of the makeshift aisle, she saw the Chandlers. It had been hard talking to them right before the ceremony began. She hadn't seen them since the time they'd picked Sandy up from camp, when she and Sandy were thirteen. Mr. Chandler looked older, more weathered, and uncomfortable in his suit. Mrs. Chandler was slim and blond, and Dawn could see traces of Sandy in her mother's features.

Brent caught her eye. She rolled her eyes, a subtle protest to the mayor's long-winded speech, and Brent grinned. Dawn kept remembering the night before, when he showed up at her door, saying, "My family's holed up in a hotel downtown, but I've managed to escape. Can I come in?"

Laughing, Dawn threw her arms around him. "You should have brought them along."

143

"Are you nuts? I've been plotting my escape all afternoon."

They went down to the rec room and settled on the sofa. He wanted to hear every word about her hospital stay. She wanted to know all about college. Haltingly, he told her about a girl he was dating. She was glad for him, and said so.

Then he took her hand and said, "I'll never forget Christmas. The talk we had that night about my sister, the things you gave me . . . I took them to the campus with me and sometimes I take them out and hold them. It's like she's there in the room with me."

Dawn touched Brent's cheek. "Sandy's the glue that holds us together," she said, knowing it was true.

"I care about you," Brent said.

"And I feel the same way about you," she replied.

"Will you be a camp counselor next summer?" he asked.

"I made up my mind at Marlee's funeral that I would. And you?"

"I'm not sure." He looked long and deep into her eyes, put his arms around her and hugged her tightly. "I'll never forget you, Dawn."

"You'd better not."

He kissed her lightly and left. She went to bed feeling as if a chapter in her life had closed.

Now, looking into Brent's face, she knew the past was truly over.

". . . speaker, Miss Dawn Rochelle."

Dawn jumped at the sound of her name. The audience burst into applause. She took a deep breath, picked up the bag and walked to the front of the stage.

"It's a real honor to be up here," she began, glad her voice didn't crack. "Marlee and her grandmother meant a lot to me. I'm just sorry they can't be here with us today."

The audience murmured and Dawn forged ahead. "I got leukemia when I was thirteen. In the hospital and at camp, I met others who also had cancer. We became great friends. Forever friends." She saw Mr. and Mrs. Chandler take each other's hand.

"Many of them are gone now." Dawn held her head high. "But I'm still here. I'm still alive. And according to my doctors, many of the kids who come to this new cancer clinic to be treated will be alive twenty—even thirty—years from now.

"So I brought some things to put in this

145

capsule in the hope that when it's opened a hundred years from now, people will see them and ask, 'What was cancer? Did people really die from it?'"

Dawn saw her mother dab her eyes with a tissue. "These things will remind them that people did die, but they will never be forgotten." She opened the bag, reached in, and pulled out the newspaper from the day the new cancer wing was announced. "I thought they might want to read the news of the day, to see what was important to us."

Dawn noticed people in the audience nodding and smiling, and she continued. "And a friend of mine made a cassette of today's top hits, so kids from tomorrow can talk about our weird taste in music." A ripple of laughter went through the listeners.

"I'm also including some items entrusted to me by my two most special friends. From Marlee Hodges, a letter she wrote to me before she died. She knew she was dying, but she was no longer afraid. And she asked that we carry on for her. And from Sandy Chandler, a page from her Bible. The verse says: 'For everything there is a season . . . A time to live and a time to die.'" She looked up. "Nobody gets to pick their time to die, but living every day to the max is something we all get to do." Dawn took a deep breath to control the slight quiver that had crept into her voice.

"And I'm putting in my personal diary. In this diary, I wrote down all my thoughts and feelings about having cancer. And I wrote about watching my friends die, one by one." Dawn saw Rob nod with approval, and Katie wipe her cheek.

"Also, I'm burying Mr. Ruggers." She pulled out her old, rumpled teddy bear, with its one missing eye and bald spots. "He's been loved a lot, but I figure it's time that he had a long rest. Maybe some kid from the future will love him as much as I have." She gently placed the tattered bear into the box on top of the other things.

Her hand trembled as she removed the final item from the sack. "And last of all, I want to put in this box of ashes from the bonfire at cancer camp. We're supposed to bring the ashes back each year and sprinkle them onto the new fire, for the kids who can't come back, for the ones who've died. But I think they belong in this capsule to remind people that we all eventually turn to ashes, even if we don't have cancer." She picked up the now-empty bag and said into the microphone, "So that's about it. I want to say thank you for giving me this privilege. Thank you for helping us win this war."

People began to applaud, then to stand. She felt a lump clog her throat and tears mist her eyes. She gazed out at the audience, at the faces of the people she loved most in the world—her family, her friends, Sandy's family. All at once, through the din of the applause, she heard birds singing in the trees. Their song, new every morning, gave her a special sense of peace.

Twenty

THE remainder of the ceremony moved quickly. Dr. Douglas dug up a spadeful of dirt while cameras clicked. The time capsule box was taken away to be permanently sealed. It would be buried by the construction crew, who would start the excavation on the new building Monday morning. Then it was announced that refreshments were being served in the hospital lobby.

People swarmed around Dawn as she made her way into the hospital. Reporters shoved mikes into her face and asked for more comments. Once inside the lobby, she grabbed a cup of punch, but before she could take a sip, the Chandlers came up to her.

"Thank you for remembering our little girl," Mr. Chandler said.

"She was my best friend. I'll never forget her," Dawn replied.

Mrs. Chandler opened her purse. "I found this in a drawer and had a copy made for you." She handed Dawn a photograph. It was a snapshot of Sandy and Dawn at camp that Mr. Chandler had taken. The two of them had their arms around each other and were mugging for the camera. Their balding heads were covered with scarves, and Sandy held Mr. Ruggers under her arm.

Dawn stared at the picture, trying to fight the tears that were springing to her eyes. How young she and Sandy looked at thirteen! And how very happy—in spite of having cancer. "Thank you," she said. "I'll treasure this always." She slipped it into the purse that was hanging from her shoulder.

Rhonda rushed over, all smiles. "Your speech was *so* fab! I mean it, Dawn, I had a huge lump in my throat the whole time." Rhonda's gaze darted to one side. "Oops. Cute guy alert to our left. I'd better go check this out."

Dawn shook her head as she watched Rhonda scurry away. Her parents and Rob and Katie came up and hugged her. "When are we going bridesmaid's dress shopping?" Dawn asked Katie.

"Is that all you can think of at a time

like this?" Katie asked, grinning.

Dawn smiled back. "Yep! Let's go next weekend! Promise?"

Rob slugged her arm playfully. "I'm proud of you, Squirt. How'd you get to be such a good speechmaker?"

"It's in my blood," she joked, and they all groaned.

Finally, the crowd thinned, the reporters and cameramen left, and the dignitaries vanished into expensive cars. Dawn leaned against a wall, sapped by the crazy tangle of emotions that had been pouring through her. "Tired?" a voice asked.

She turned and faced Jake. She'd forgotten he was there.

"Yes, but it's a good tired."

He took her empty punch cup and placed it on a table. "Come on. I'll take you home." She glanced around for her parents.

"I asked your mom and dad if I could drive you," Jake explained. "They said it would be all right."

"That was nice of you."

"Hey, I'm a nice guy." He grinned. "Besides, I'm not about to let some hot-shot college guy ace me out."

"Brent? He's just a friend. I didn't know you cared."

"I care, all right," Jake said. He took a deep breath. "And I'm sorry I yelled at you in the hospital. That was no way to treat a friend."

"I guess I needed it," she said, feeling her mouth go dry. "Pity parties aren't my usual style."

"Well after hearing your speech today, I'm able to see some things through your eyes. I can't imagine watching my friends die the way you have. And I can't imagine how you deal with knowing it could happen to you too."

Dawn shrugged. "I really try not to dwell on that part, Jake. No matter how down I feel, I try to concentrate on living, not dying."

"Well, even though I'm sorry for the way I said it, I'm not entirely sorry for what I said. You do make me feel like an outsider sometimes, as if I don't belong in the cancer part of your life."

Dawn experienced a pang of guilt. Is that what she had been doing to him? "I never meant to make you feel like an outcast because you're healthy. It's just so hard trying to live in two worlds."

"When we were in seventh grade and the teacher told the class that you had leukemia, I felt really rotten. It scared me. I felt sorry for you, but I didn't know how to tell you."

"That's part of the problem," Dawn said. "People like me, who are sick or hurting, don't want pity. We just want to be accepted."

"I stopped feeling pity for you that day at the school carnival. I wanted you to notice me. That's why I volunteered to go into the dunk tank."

If he only knew how much she'd noticed him! "I couldn't believe it when you showed up here at Hardy this year."

"Me either. But I'm glad we moved back to Columbus. And I'm glad I got to know you again. I wasn't sure how to treat you at first. I wasn't sure you'd want to be around some guy you'd known since the fifth grade."

"I felt the same way," she said. "I'd changed so much and been through so much while you were gone. I didn't want you to feel as if you owed me anything just because you'd known me for a long time."

His voice became low and soft. "I always liked you, Dawn. And I have a feeling I always will."

Her heart skipped a beat, and she felt so

giddy and lightweight that she thought she might float off the floor. "I always liked you too."

For a minute they stood staring into one another's eyes. Finally, Jake said, "We'd better get going."

They had only walked a few steps when Dawn stopped. "I just thought of something I need to do before I leave," she said. "Will you come with me?"

"Lead the way."

She crossed to the elevator and punched the button for the top floor. She and Jake rode up in silence and when the doors slid open, they stepped off into a deserted section of offices.

"Where are we?" Jake wanted to know.

"Follow me." She led the way past a bank of windows, down the dimly lit hall, and stopped in front of the mural of the Tree of Life. Its long branches and green leaves seemed alive.

"Cool," Jake commented. "Whose names are on the leaves?"

"Survivors. They're people who've beaten the odds against cancer. They're part of a support group that I'm going to join."

He studied the tree carefully. "Where's your name?"

Dawn took a deep breath. "It's not there yet."

He glanced at her quickly. "Why not?"

"No good reason. Come on, pick a leaf for me."

Jake pointed to a leaf near the top of its furthermost branches. Dawn dug in her purse until she found a felt-tip pen. She stepped forward, took a deep breath, and wrote her name in bold black strokes. "There. What do you think?"

"I think it looks terrific."

She stepped away from the wall and looked up at him. Jake reached out and gently raised her chin with his forefinger and gazed into her eyes. "You know that old saying 'This is the first day of the rest of your life'? I always thought it was kind of corny, but now it seems to fit. What do you think, Dawn? Is that true?"

She felt her heart pound at jackhammer speed. *The rest of her life!* No one ever knew what the future held—even kids who never got leukemia. Perhaps her cancer would be permanently cured. Maybe she'd go to medical school and become a doctor and help others, like Dr. Ben had done. Maybe she'd get married. And maybe she'd be able to have children someday in spite

155

of the grim prognosis. Maybe life was for living. She said, "Yes, Jake Macka. It's true."

He brushed his lips lightly across hers, then tucked her under his arm, against his side. "Then let's go live it."

She hooked her arm around his waist, and together they walked down the deserted hallway toward the light streaming through the windows.

About the Author

Lurlene McDaniel lives in Chattanooga, Tennessee, and is a favorite author of young people all over the country. Her best-selling books about kids overcoming problems such as cancer, diabetes, and the death of a parent or sibling draw a wide response from her readers. Lurlene says that the best compliment she can receive is having a reader tell her, "Your story was so interesting that I couldn't put it down!" To Lurlene, the most important thing is writing an uplifting story that helps the reader to look at life from a different perspective.

Six Months to Live, the first of the best-selling books about Dawn Rochelle and her courageous fight against cancer, was placed in a time capsule at the Library of Congress in Washington, D.C. The capsule is scheduled to be opened in the year 2089.

Other Willowisp Press books by Lurlene McDaniel include *If I Should Die Before I Wake*, *Why Did She Have to Die?*, *When Dreams Shatter*, and *Mother, Please Don't Die*.